As the pupils scrambled out of the classroom for the playground, Mrs Sherry and Mrs Clegg exchanged despairing looks. It had been hard work getting the pupils of Barton Wood interested in Roman society and customs; and Mr Higgins had made great progress with his Victorian project.

Now it looked as if those two subjects might be forgotten by what they both realized would probably be one of the main topics of conversation in the school playground for the rest of the day. Neither of them would have been surprised if, by the end of the afternoon, someone came up to them and asked if it was true that the school was haunted.

Mrs Sherry shook her head and fanned herself with the borrowed Victorian fan she was taking to Mr Higgins's class. Puppies and ghosts! She didn't know when she was well off!

Nigel Robinson

three seven eleven:
Barton Wood For Ever

based on the Granada Television series
of the same name,
written by Bernard Ashley, Chris Ashley and Marvin Close

PUFFIN BOOKS

PUFFIN BOOKS

Published by the Penguin Group
Penguin Books Ltd, 27 Wrights Lane, London w8 5tz, England
Penguin Books USA Inc., 375 Hudson Street, New York, New York 10014, USA
Penguin Books Australia Ltd, Ringwood, Victoria, Australia
Penguin Books Canada Ltd, 10 Alcorn Avenue, Toronto, Ontario, Canada m4v 3b2
Penguin Books (NZ) Ltd, 182–190 Wairau Road, Auckland 10, New Zealand

Penguin Books Ltd, Registered Offices: Harmondsworth, Middlesex, England

First published 1994
1 3 5 7 9 10 8 6 4 2

three seven eleven: Barton Wood For Ever copyright © Granada Television, 1994
Text copyright © Nigel Robinson, 1994
All rights reserved

The moral right of the author has been asserted

Filmset by Datix International Limited, Bungay, Suffolk
Printed in England by Clays Ltd, St Ives plc
Set in 11/13 pt Monophoto Garamond

Chapter One

Miranda Pudsey watched her next-door-but-one neighbour Joe Kerton as he tramped through his back garden to the dustbin. Joe didn't know that Miranda was spying on him, but then staying out of sight was one of Miranda's specialities.

More than once she'd sneaked out from under the nose of Mrs Sherry or Mrs Clegg at Barton Wood School, and it had taken half the teaching staff most of the morning to track her down.

Miranda knew that some of the teachers at school called her a difficult kid; she also knew that she could run rings around any of them when she wanted to. The only thing was, that, for most of the time, she couldn't be bothered to: it was much more fun playing with the younger children at school, helping them with paintings and drawings. At least they needed her, unlike her parents.

She glanced back towards her house and winced as she heard the angry cries of her mum and dad. Miranda had come out into the garden to save herself from the inevitable fall-out from one of their many argy-bargies.

Still, she reflected as she watched Joe go about his business, things were improving; they were only hurling insults and abuse at each other this morning. Last week it had been the best crockery.

Anyway, she had more important things on her mind at the moment, like keeping warm on this cold winter's day, and finding out why Joe was acting so secretively in his own back garden. Maybe he was concealing a body, she thought idly; now, that would brighten up her morning no end.

Joe looked around nervously, to make sure that no one was watching, and then took an empty cardboard box from out of his jacket and dumped it into the dustbin. From her hiding-place behind the fence, Miranda could see that it had once contained a rubber toy for a puppy.

He was also carrying a small, black, refuse bag, and now he split the bag open, spreading its contents over the cardboard box. Miranda had seen enough detective stories on telly to know what he was doing: covering up the evidence, she realized.

'Cold, innit, Joe?' she piped up, and sprang from behind the fence like a jack-in-the-box. To her delight, Joe almost jumped out of his skin.

'How long have you been there?' he asked.

Miranda shrugged. 'Ages,' she said, and glanced meaningfully over at her house.

Joe nodded. He couldn't blame Miranda for wanting to be out of that combat zone. Mr and Mrs Pudsey had been going at it hammer and tongs for the past twenty minutes and it wasn't even half-seven in the morning yet.

'You want a cup of tea?' he asked, offering the classic British remedy in times of crisis.

'Ta.'

Joe nodded over to the Pudsey house. 'Shall I go and tell 'em?' he asked.

Miranda raised her eyes heavenwards and sighed. Joe was a nice enough bloke, and as the new school caretaker at Barton Wood, she reckoned he was just about as good as the last one. But sometimes he had about as much sense as salmon going for a dip in the Manchester Ship Canal.

'You wanna die?' she asked simply.

'Maybe not, eh?' Joe sighed with relief, and led the way up to the back kitchen, where he could hear his wife singing along to the early-morning show on Piccadilly.

'What was that puppy thing you chucked in the dustbin?' Miranda asked loudly.

Joe put his finger to his lips and tried to shut her up. All he succeeded in doing was to intrigue Miranda even more. If this was a secret, she wanted to be in on it.

'You having one of them puppies from Swainsgate?' she demanded, referring to the school secretary at Barton Wood.

'*Mrs* Swainsgate!' he corrected her, and grinned.

'Well, are you?'

'I said shush!' Joe grinned and placed a hand over her mouth, which he withdrew a second later with a yelp. 'Ow!'

Miranda smiled up at him sweetly, and licked her lips.

'Not only dogs bite,' she laughed, and swanked into the back kitchen of the Kerton household.

As Miranda enjoyed a hot sweet cuppa in the Kertons' back kitchen, Nicky Power was leaning nonchalantly against the gatepost of his mate Lee Rayner's house. In his hands he held a note which he had been reading over and over on the way up to the Rayner home. He had a cocky grin on his face.

There was, however, no grin on Lee's face as he shambled out of the front door and slammed it shut. He was scowling darkly, as if he'd just come a cropper on his last maths test.

He walked sullenly past Nicky, who ran after him.

'What's up with you?' Nicky asked. He caught up with him and they walked down the road together.

Lee shrugged. 'Don't have to grin all over my face going to scudding school!' he said sullenly. He glowered at his friend: what did he have to be so chuffed about this early in the morning, he wondered.

Nicky chuckled, and waved the piece of paper in front of Lee. 'You'd be grinning if you was me,' he said. 'I got my plans!'

Lee wasn't impressed: he'd heard it all before. Nicky seemed to have a plan a day, and all with the same daft object in mind. 'Helping your dad escape from prison?' he asked, and added sarcastically: 'Hang on, I'll phone the *Sun*!'

'It's early days yet,' Nicky said, determined not to let his friend put him off. 'Part one.'

Lee shook his head. If he wanted to hear a fairy story, he could hear one in Cleggie's class.

'Early days?' he scoffed. 'He'll have done his time in the nick before you get him out!'

'Don't you believe it!' Nicky said, and waved the note in Lee's face once more. 'If this works I'm on course. Part one – get the dog. Part two – get the dog food!'

Lee stared at Nicky, thinking his mate had lost a few brain cells somewhere along the way this morning. He was about to say as much, when they spotted a group of their friends and joined them.

Much to Lee's despair they were also gabbing on about dogs. What was it about bundles of fluff and teeth, he wondered, that made grown kids go all gooey and sentimental?

Esi Mensah, the Ghanaian girl who was in Lee's Year Six class, obviously felt the same. For the past ten minutes Lyn Lawrence had been boring her rigid with all her chatter about dogs, dogs, and more dogs.

'My mum said I could have one when we moved,' Lyn declared excitedly, and waved her own piece of paper in front of Esi's face. 'See. She wrote me this note.' She shuddered with anticipation. 'I can't wait to get it home. We're going to take it in turns giving it walks.' She glanced behind her at her brother Liam, who was chatting with Kate Mulligan. 'Everyone's arguing about who's going to be first.'

'They won't let me have one,' said Esi sadly.

'But you were on the list!' Lyn protested.

She remembered sneaking a look at the list Mrs Swainsgate had drawn up with all those she thought capable of bringing up one of her newly-born puppies. Esi's name had definitely been there.

'*They* won't write the letter,' said Esi. It was quite clear who *They* were. 'It's like wanting the end of the rainbow wanting a dog in our house.'

Much to her dismay she saw that Nicky also had a note scrunched up in his hand. He came over and started making idiotic dog-noises at her.

'Stupid dogs!' she cried angrily. 'Isn't there anything else?'

'Too right!' agreed Lee. He was glad to see that at least someone today was acting with a bit of sense.

As they walked down the road, they passed by Roberta James's house. Roberta was just leaving with her younger brother Darren, and Nicky and the others ran up to them.

'You got yours?' asked Nicky, brandishing his note in the air again. Lee shook his head: the way Nicky was acting you'd think that he had the title deeds to Buckingham Palace instead of a scrappy piece of paper saying that he could have a puppy.

'Got my what?' Roberta said, pretending not to know what Nicky was going on about.

'Your note for a dog,' Lyn explained.

'I decided I didn't want one,' she said, all superior. 'A dog's for life, you know, not just for now.'

Esi nodded her head wisely: it looked as if *They* had put their big parental foot down in Roberta's house as well.

Nicky continued to wave his note about and Roberta snatched it from his hand and began to read it. 'Your mother never wrote this!' she said.

'No, she never wrote it cos it's typed, brainbox,' he replied quickly. 'But she signed it!'

'It's appalling typing,' Roberta said disapprovingly. Roberta liked to have everything all neat and tidy. That was one of the reasons why she was so good at playing chess, her teachers had said.

'Some people do things appalling, but they still do them,' Lyn pointed out. 'Like my mum's cooking – yuk! yuk!'

Nicky grabbed his note from Roberta; she promptly snatched it back. There was something distinctly strange abut this, she decided.

She began to read aloud from the letter: '"Dear

Mrs *Swinesgate*, I whereby allow you to give Nicky a puppy to take into custody. Yours truthfully, Mrs Power."'

She looked disbelievingly at Nicky and handed him back his note. 'Is that supposed to be English?' she asked.

Nicky shrugged, while Lee tittered behind him.

'Your mum never wrote that – and she never typed it,' Roberta said firmly.

Nicky said nothing. He just put the note back into his pocket. He sneaked a look at Lee and whispered, 'She never signed it neither. I'm a "scratcher"!'

'You got fleas?'

'Scratcher's a pro name for a forger,' Nicky said proudly. 'I'm good at it!'

'And you reckon that forgery's going to fool Swainsgate?'

'Too right,' was Nicky's confident answer. After all, Swainsgate was only the school secretary: it wasn't like she was Inspector Morse or anything. 'She won't be up to this!'

Lee couldn't understand why Nicky was so dead-set keen on having a puppy. He could understand even less just how a daft puppy could help spring Nicky's dad from the nick.

He turned back and spotted Liam Lawrence and Kate Mulligan. They were talking about the school's forthcoming Victorian project. Mrs Sherry, the headteacher, had asked them all to bring in examples of the way people lived their life in Barton Wood way back in the nineteenth century. It sounded interesting, he decided; well, at least, more interesting than boring old puppies and Nicky's brain-dead idea to break into Strangeways and pull the escape job of the century.

Joe carried a large cardboard box into Mrs Swainsgate's office. He was dressed in his caretaker's overalls, but he held the box like a waiter in a grand hotel bringing in the dish of the day. From inside the box came the yapping sound of four puppies.

Finding nowhere to put the box down, he took it into Mrs Sherry's adjoining office, where he placed it carefully on the headteacher's desk.

'There you go!' he said, and peered over the rim of the box to see the excited and inquisitive faces of four tiny puppies.

He then frowned and took a tissue from the box on the windowsill, which he used to mop up the mess that one of the dogs had already made on its straw and paper bedding.

Standing behind him in the doorway was Mrs Swainsgate, who was busy taking notes from Kate, Lyn and Liam, and Nicky. They had followed her from the moment her car had pulled into the carpark, with the puppies in the back.

'Can I have a boy?' Kate asked eagerly. 'My mum said to get a boy if possible.'

Mrs Swainsgate smiled and glanced at Kate's note. 'We'll sort out dogs and bitches in a minute,' she promised, and took a series of postcards from her shoulderbag.

'First things first,' she announced importantly, and read out the list of instructions which she had written on each of the postcards. 'These are your first dos and don'ts. You need a litter tray, a box or a basket for a bed, two bowls – one for food and one for water – a collar and a lead. Some toys would also be a good idea.'

'Scalextric do, miss?' chirped up Nicky as Mrs Swainsgate started to hand out the postcards.

'Rubber bones or balls,' she said, and gave him a withering look. 'I hope you're serious about this, Nicky. Have you got a note?'

Nicky nodded and handed the forged note over to Mrs Swainsgate, who looked at him suspiciously.

'Did your mother type this?' she asked.

'Not gonna be my dad, is it?'

'He's in the nick,' Lyn added helpfully.

Mrs Swainsgate flushed red with embarrassment and hurriedly handed the note back to Nicky without reading it.

'*May* I come in?' asked a familiar voice.

Mrs Sherry was standing patiently in the secretary's office, looking at the crowd of schoolchildren who were blocking the entrance to *her* office. She was carrying a pile of letters and parcels which had arrived in the morning post. As Mrs Swainsgate parted the crowd of children, Mrs Sherry passed through into her office and looked around.

'And where do you think I am supposed to work?' she said frostily to Joe, who was bending over the cardboard box, playing with the puppies, the way someone might with a tiny baby.

He looked up as she came in and stood to attention. Mrs Sherry had a way of making people do that.

Joe rubbed his chin thoughtfully. 'Now there's a tough one,' he said, as one of the puppies cheekily peeked its head over the rim of the cardboard.

'Dogs!' Mrs Sherry despaired. When she had come to Barton Wood a year ago, she thought she'd been taking over a school, not a blessed pet shop!

'Yeah!' said Joe enthusiastically, and playfully scratched the ear of one of the puppies. 'That's my fellow there. Norton's his name.'

Mrs Sherry looked down into the cardboard box. She had to admit that the puppies did look rather cute.

'Norton?' she asked. 'That's no name for a dog!'

'If it's good enough for the finest motorcycle ever built, then it's good enough for him,' Joe said defensively.

'Are you having one of these then – instead of a motorbike?' she asked.

'That's a moot point,' he admitted. 'I said I'd be waiting in the wings if young Esi got turned down.'

Mrs Sherry smiled to herself; she knew that deep down Joe was what her mother might have called a 'big softy'. She put the post down on an empty chair and sniffed. There was a peculiar smell in the air.

'It doesn't smell like a new school any more,' she said, and shook her head sadly.

Joe looked guiltily back at the cardboard box: he'd smelt it too, and, what was more, he had a fair idea where it was coming from.

Mrs Sherry was about to press the matter further when the phone rang. She looked out into the secretary's office. Mrs Swainsgate was still reading out her list of dos and don'ts to the children.

'Could that possibly be the phone ringing?' Mrs Sherry asked in a loud and sarcastic voice.

Mrs Swainsgate didn't hear her and, finally giving

in to the inevitable, Mrs Sherry handed the puppy box to Joe. She sat down grumpily at her desk to answer the phone just as it stopped ringing.

She indicated the puppy box. 'Your office,' she told Joe. 'Norton and the rest of the mopeds.'

'Oh, OK.' Joe carried the puppy box out of her office and towards the far door. He was followed by the children, each of them eagerly looking into the box.

When they had gone Mrs Sherry looked around her office and wrinkled her nose. That peculiar smell was still there. It smelt exactly like . . .

Oh no! she thought, they couldn't have, not in here . . .

She was about to look down at the floor, when Mrs Swainsgate walked in. The school secretary wrinkled her nose too, and looked nervously around the office.

'Is there anything wrong?' asked the secretary.

Mrs Sherry stood up and gave Mrs Swainsgate a look which clearly meant, *We'll talk about this later*. What she said was, 'Nothing at all, Olive. Whatever gave you that idea?'

Mrs Sherry walked out of her office, with a selection of the early-morning post, leaving Mrs Swainsgate to cope as best she could with that smell – whatever it might be.

Chapter Two

Safe in the staffroom, away from the stink that had invaded her office, Mrs Sherry sat down to open her mail.

Most of today's post was what a normal primary school could expect. There were photocopied circulars in their distinctive brown-paper envelopes from the Department of Education and Science; there were letters from parents regarding the various pursuits of their children; there was even a letter from Councillor Bamber, one of the school's governors, assuring Mrs Sherry that he was delighted with the work that she and her colleagues were putting into the new school. Mrs Sherry nodded knowingly: such a letter probably meant that Len Bamber, a hearty and cheerful middle-aged man, would be coming over to check up on them very soon. He meant well, but whenever he *did* turn up at Barton Wood he tended to throw the whole school into chaos. She made a mental note to warn the other teachers, although as the deputy head, Jack Higgins, said, he and his fellow teachers were always on Bamber alert.

Mrs Sherry ripped open a brown-paper parcel which had a Manchester postmark. She smiled as she saw what was inside the parcel, wrapped up in a protective covering. It was a delicate Victorian silk fan, which she was borrowing from a local elegant dress shop. She could have done with it in the office earlier, she thought; however, it was going to be ideal for Barton Wood's forthcoming Victorian Day.

The Victorian Day had originally been the idea of Jack Higgins. Remembering his own schooldays, when history had been about as interesting as a day out in the rain watching Wigan Athletic play rugby, he'd wanted to enliven his history lessons for his younger pupils. He had hit on the idea of holding a Victorian project, where everyone was encouraged to bring into school an everyday item from the nineteenth century. It could be anything at all, he had told his class, and everyone had responded, some more enthusiastically than others. Mandy Willis, for instance, had brought in an old soda bottle which had belonged to her gran, balancing it carefully on her lap as she wheeled herself in through the school gates in her wheelchair.

Darren James, however, had intended to bring in a copy of *Oliver Twist*, the famous Charles Dickens novel about the life of a young boy in nineteenth-century London, but had forgotten at the last minute. Darren was becoming more and more forgetful these days. Mr Higgins had made a mental note to discuss the matter with Darren's sister Roberta when he had the time.

Mr Higgins's idea had been so successful that he had even managed to persuade Mrs Sherry to get the rest of the school involved. As she waved the elegant Victorian fan in front of her, Mrs Sherry looked forward to the Victorian Day with a mixture of dread and pleasure. It might prove to be fun having all the members of the school dressed up for the day as Victorians.

She started to wonder what she might wear herself. Mr Higgins had said that he was going to dress up as Benjamin Disraeli, the famous Prime Minister, and Mrs Sherry knew that she couldn't let the teaching side down by appearing on the day in her usual smart, sensible suit. But she didn't know whether she had the nerve to wear her Victorian costume to school. After all, it was just something she had made for a fancy-dress party a few years ago and it was a little over the top.

While Mrs Sherry was worrying about the Victorian age, Mrs Clegg's mind was occupied even further back in time. The walls of her Year Six classroom were covered from top to bottom with charts and illustrations of life in Britain nearly two thousand years ago, when almost the entire island of Britannia had been occupied by the Romans.

There were charts showing the courses of the Roman roads, linking towns all the way from Londinium (London) in the south, to nearby Mancunium (Manchester). They went right the way up to Hadrian's wall on the Scottish border, which was where the Romans met their match in the shape of the fearsome Picts.

Standing guard in a corner, by a collection of models of Roman villas, was a life-sized Roman centurion – or rather a shop dummy on castors, dressed up to look like one. The dummy had been lent to Mrs Clegg by the owner of yet another elegant dress shop; she just hoped that none of her pupils looked too closely at her Roman centurion, or else they would discover that it wasn't a male dummy after all!

Not that they seemed to be paying much attention to the dummy at the moment. A good two-thirds of the class were watching, fascinated, as she used the overhead projector to show one local map after another on the whiteboard on the wall. As she progressed through the maps, she was able to take them back on a trip through time, showing how Barton Wood and its surrounding area had changed over the centuries.

There was Barton Wood school and its neighbouring housing estate on the first map, and, as she replaced the acetate map with one of the area just eighteen months earlier, they could all see the fields on which the new buildings had been constructed.

Mrs Clegg took them even further back in time, pointing out with the shadow of her pencil the old coal-mines just off the main Pennington Road, which were in operation until only twenty or so years ago.

Finally she brought them to the times of the Romans themselves, and on her last map indicated the probable location of a Roman villa which used to stand on the site. She drew her pencil along the route of the Pennington Road.

'The Pennington Road was originally built by the Romans themselves,' she explained. Thirty pupils instantly imagined thousands of Romans marching along the same road they took to school every day.

'On the side of it – probably about here,' she said, and pointed with the pencil again, 'would have been the home of a governor . . .'

'What? Like Mr Bamber?' asked Lyn. Somehow she couldn't quite imagine the bluff and hearty school governor walking around dressed only in a toga and a tatty pair of leather sandals.

Mrs Clegg shook her head. 'A Roman governor was someone important in the region,' she explained. 'He probably lived somewhere near us, or perhaps over towards Turnpike Lane.'

'I live near Turnpike Lane,' piped up Paul Haines.

'Oooh, very posh,' said Miranda.

'So why aren't the walls of the villa in our garden?' Paul asked, only half-flippantly. In fact he was beginning to find the whole subject really interesting.

'That's because the Roman Pennington Road is two or three metres deeper than our modern road,' answered Mrs Clegg.

'Think of all that dust over the years,' giggled Esi. Her mother, who always tried to keep their own house spotlessly clean, would have had a fit.

'That's right, Esi,' continued Mrs Clegg as she explained how, over the years, the level of the land had risen considerably. 'If the ghosts of a legion of Roman soldiers marched past the front of the school today, then all you would see would be the tops of their helmets.'

'*Ghosts!*' Kenny cried out. Now this sounded really interesting; much better than the type of houses a whole bunch of dead and boring Romans lived in. 'Do ghosts really march past here?'

As he said that, the dummy of the Roman centurion came off its castors and started to fall to the ground. Mrs Clegg darted over to catch it, just as Mrs Sherry walked into the classroom, carrying a register in her hand. She watched on, amused, as the teacher struggled with the heavy shop dummy.

'And what's this? A waltz or the fight of the gladiators?' she asked wryly.

'It's come off its castors,' puffed Mrs Clegg.

'It's a ghost, miss!' Miranda decided gleefully.

'He started coming for us.'

'He did – I heard him moan – *oooooooooooer*!'

Mrs Sherry turned sternly on the class. 'Don't be silly,' she said as she went over to help the struggling Mrs Clegg return the dummy to an upright position. 'There's no such things as ghosts!'

The look on the faces of the class seemed to prove that very few of them actually believed her. Mrs Sherry slammed the register on the desk. 'Let's have an end to all this nonsense, shall we?' she said. 'This is the way hysteria starts to grow.'

'We're gonna plant some of that in our garden,' offered Lyn, and several of her schoolfriends started to snigger.

Mrs Clegg, who had finally managed to stand her centurion upright, gave her a withering look and then dismissed the class.

As the pupils scrambled out of the classroom for the playground, Mrs Sherry and Mrs Clegg exchanged despairing looks. It had been hard work getting the pupils of Barton Wood interested in Roman society and customs; and Mr Higgins had made great progress with his Victorian project.

Now it looked as if those two subjects might be forgotten by what they both realized would probably be one of the main topics of conversation in the school playground for the rest of the day. Neither of them would have been surprised if, by the end of the afternoon, someone came up to them and asked if it was true that the school was haunted.

Mrs Sherry shook her head and fanned herself with

the borrowed Victorian fan she was taking to Mr Higgins's class. Puppies and ghosts! She didn't know when she was well off!

'We're going shopping tomorrow, OK?' Nicky whispered to Kenny and Lee later that afternoon. They were all sitting together at a corner table, making copied Roman pots out of Alloplast moulds. At the other end of the room Mrs Clegg was reading out a story to the rest of the class.

Kenny looked at his mate strangely. 'What we going shopping for then?' he asked.

'Ain't got no dosh anyway,' said Lee, and turned his pockets inside out as if to prove it.

'Don't need dosh, not how I go shopping, scud,' said Nicky mysteriously, and tapped the side of his nose in a secretive gesture. 'Part two – get the dog food!'

Before Lee or Kenny had had the chance to ask Nicky exactly what he was talking about, Mrs Clegg told them to stop making such a noise. Nicky smiled a cheeky grin and nodded down at the pot he was making.

'Wasn't me, miss, I was pottering!'

'It could've been a ghost,' Lee suggested in what he thought was a dark and spooky tone of voice.

Mrs Clegg frowned. 'I do not want to hear another word about the ghost!' she said sternly.

She instantly regretted her words as Esi shivered and said, 'So there *is* a ghost then!'

Mrs Clegg raised her eyes heavenwards and sighed: Mrs Sherry had been right. By the end of today the rumour that Barton Wood was haunted by the ghosts of an entire Roman legion would be all around the school. Admitting defeat, she returned to reading her story, and Nicky, Lee and Kenny went back to their modelling.

Nicky looked anxiously at his watch. 'It won't be long now,' he whispered.

'Before what?' asked Kenny.

'Getting the dog off Swainsgate,' Nicky replied excitedly. 'First we get the dog, and then the food, and then –' He glanced around to see if anyone was looking but the rest of the class were listening to Mrs Clegg's story. 'And then we spring my dad from prison!'

After having locked up the school for the evening Joe Kerton glumly walked along the pathway to his house, his hands rammed deep in his trouser pockets. He idly kicked a stone on the pathway and sighed. He was acting like a sulky kid, he knew that, but he didn't care: today must surely count as one of the most disappointing days of his life.

He had really wanted one of Mrs Swainsgate's puppies, but when he had told his wife Jackie about it at lunchtime, she had expressly forbidden it.

He had been brutally disappointed: he'd thought that she would have liked some company around the house during the daytime, when he was at work: after all, listening to Radio Piccadilly every hour of the day wasn't exactly the most stimulating of pleasures. And still Jackie had said no, before rushing off for a mysterious appointment in town. Joe sighed. Women! he thought. Who understood them?

It was Miranda he'd felt most sorry for: the poor

kid must have been gutted. She'd hoped to come over every night and every morning before school to play with the puppy.

Joe had told her that the puppy would really be hers, but that it would be staying at the Kertons' as a sort of lodger since Miranda's parents wouldn't allow a dog in their house. She'd so much looked forward to that puppy, and had even called it Stevie after her dead baby brother. And now there was going to be no puppy.

What had upset Joe the most was knowing that by now Mrs Swainsgate had handed out the other puppies to Nicky, Lyn and Liam, and Kate. He wondered who'd be putting up little Stevie for the night. Probably Mrs Swainsgate would take him home with her again.

As he entered his house by the back kitchen door he didn't see Miranda, who had been hiding in the shadows. There was a sneaky look on her face.

She grinned. People might feel sorry for her at times, and some of the grown-ups might pat her patronizingly on the head and say, 'What a poor child,' but Miranda knew that she always got her own way in the end.

So what if Jackie *had* said that she and Joe couldn't share a puppy? Miranda would find a way round that, as she always did. She'd set her heart on Stevie and nothing was going to take him away from her.

Underneath her cardigan the puppy slept softly in Miranda's arms. She had taken it from the puppy box just before Mrs Swainsgate had arrived to hand them out. When the secretary had appeared she had naturally assumed that Joe had already taken the puppy.

She followed Joe up the path and knocked on the kitchen door before opening it. There was a big grin on her face as she showed Jackie and Joe the puppy.

'I brought him for us,' she said, and showed Jackie Stevie's cute little face. 'I knew you'd love him when you saw him,' she added hopefully.

Jackie's face softened, but when she spoke her tone was stern. 'Miranda, we are not having a puppy,' she said, and turned to Joe. He seemed to be more concerned with what was on the kitchen table, and there was a puzzled look on his face. Instead of his usual tea of egg and chips and a can of Coke, there was a juicy sizzling steak and a bottle of champagne.

Miranda's face became angry as she turned to Joe. 'You said you were having the dog for *me*!' She spat out the words. 'Why are you all changing your mind?'

'In this case there're reasons,' said Jackie, a little more softly now, as she realized the bitter disappointment that Miranda must be feeling.

'Yeah, Jackie's got reasons,' Joe shrugged, clearly unsure of what they were.

He tried to figure out why Jackie had gone to so much trouble to prepare such a lavish meal for him tonight. It was almost as if she was celebrating something.

Jackie turned to face her husband and patted her stomach meaningfully. 'I've got one very good reason,' she breathed. 'The best reason in the world . . . We're not having a dog because – after five years of trying – we are finally having a baby!'

It took a few seconds for what Jackie had said to sink in. Then Joe swept his wife up in his arms and hugged her. He was laughing and crying at the same time.

'I don't believe it!' he cried for joy. 'I'm having a baby! I'm having a baby!'

As the Kertons stood in the kitchen embracing, it seemed that Miranda had suddenly ceased to exist for them. Miranda's face fell, and tears appeared in the corners of her eyes.

She looked jealously up at Joe and Jackie, unable to share in their happiness. Miranda had longed to have a puppy of her own, but once again the grown-ups had let her down.

Well, they can keep their stupid baby, for all I care, she thought bitterly.

Silently Miranda dropped Stevie on to the doormat, and ran out of the Kertons' kitchen, with hot salty tears running down her cheeks. So happy were Joe and Jackie that it was a few minutes before they even noticed that she had gone.

Chapter Three

The old wooden shack on the allotments hadn't been used in years. Mould and rot crept up its inside walls whilst spiders and bugs crawled all over its mossy damp floor. It was so decrepit and rickety that it was a wonder it hadn't been blown away by the slightest breeze, or washed away in a shower. The only light came from a hole in the low roof, which also let in the rain.

But when Nicky proudly invited Kenny into it he acted as if he was opening the gates of Buckingham Palace. This was Nicky's secret hideout and he only ever allowed in people he knew he could trust and count on. It was also where he had made a bed out of some old blankets and straw for Scratch, the puppy he had been given yesterday by Mrs Swainsgate.

Kenny looked around the interior of the shed disapprovingly and wrinkled his nose at the smell, as Nicky threw down the big shoulderbag he was carrying. It landed with a heavy thud on the ground. Underneath his coat Nicky was wearing a freshly ironed shirt and – the biggest surprise of all – an awkwardly knotted tie.

'I'm visiting me old man,' Nicky said. He picked up Scratch, cuddling the puppy to his chest.

Kenny nodded, grateful that his own dad wasn't in the nick, where he could only see him once a month. Although sometimes he might just well as be, Kenny thought, for all the attention he gives me. In fact Mr

Bayfield had been behaving strangely for some days now, never seeming to spend his days off with Kenny, and always smelling of cheap aftershave. Even his grandad couldn't explain to Kenny what the matter was. Kenny wished his mum was still alive: things would have been a lot different then.

There was a coded tap at the door and it swung open to reveal Lee. He slammed the door shut behind him, and nodded at the other two, assuring them that no one had seen him enter the shack.

Nicky grunted approvingly, put Scratch down on the ground, and opened up his big bag. He took out several packets of dog biscuits and a carton of milk, then opened up his coat. Four cans of dog food tumbled to the floor, and from out of his coat sleeve he pulled a long stick of dog chocolate.

Kenny gasped. 'Where did you get all that?'

'Went shopping, didn't I?' Nicky said casually. 'And you were supposed to be there, Rayner!' he said accusingly. 'You lost your bottle now that your dad's come back?'

Lee stared at Nicky. 'No, I haven't,' he said. 'I just don't nick, that's all.'

'You *nicked* all that?' asked Kenny as Nicky poured the milk into a container and mashed the biscuits up with a rusty old fork.

Nicky sighed: sometimes Kenny Bayfield was a little too straight and innocent for his own good.

'No, I went into the shop and old man Vasisht was giving it away!' he said sarcastically, remembering how he'd swiped the cans from under Vasisht's nose when the Asian shopkeeper was gossiping away to old Albert Dawson. 'What grub did you bring, Bayfield?'

Kenny handed over the plastic carrier bag he had brought, almost apologetically. Nicky eagerly tore it open and pulled out a pack of buttered crumpets and a couple of bananas.

He looked disappointedly at Kenny, who responded with a weak, 'It's all I could get . . .'

Nicky sighed: Scratch was going to need more than this to keep his strength up if he was going to continue living in this shack. He opened one of the cans of dog food and began to spoon it into Scratch's bowl, while Kenny pointed out that Mrs Swainsgate had advised them all to avoid canned dog food if at all possible.

Nicky shook his head and stood up, smoothing down his coat, which was already spattered with mud. 'It was risky nicking all this, and I can't do it on me own every day,' he said, and added, 'You lot will have to help.'

Lee and Kenny exchanged uncomfortable glances as Nicky gave Scratch one final ruffle behind the neck, and then left the shack.

'I'm not nicking from the shop,' Kenny said, as soon as Nicky had left.

Lee didn't say anything, but just continued to watch Scratch, who was greedily scoffing up the canned dog food. He still didn't understand why Nicky had wanted a dog and how it could help spring his dad from the nick. What he did understand, however, was that it was slowly turning out to be not such a brilliant idea after all.

After they had fed Scratch, Kenny had gone back outside, to the allotment where his dad and his grandad had been working for most of the morning. Neither of them had noticed that he'd been away; they'd been far too busy working his grandad's vegetable patch. In fact, the only one who seemed to be in the slightest interested in his return was Monty, the family's old mongrel, who ran up to him yelping and yapping.

Kenny's dad grinned. 'What's up with Monty?' he asked. 'He can smell something on you, Kenny.'

Yeah, like Scratch, thought Kenny worriedly.

He wondered whether he should tell his dad about Nicky's stealing the dog food from Mr Vasisht's store. Kenny knew it was wrong. The trouble was, he realized, Nicky was his mate, and at Barton Wood the rule was that you never grassed on your mates.

'You've not started using your dad's new aftershave, have you?' asked Grandad Bayfield, and instantly regretted it as Kenny's dad shot him an angry glare.

Kenny shook his head, but it didn't help to be reminded of his dad's new change of attitude these days. New aftershave, new shirt, even a new tie. Who was he trying to impress?

Mr Bayfield began to gather up the garden tools, throwing them in the wheelbarrow which he'd take to their own allotment shed. He had to rush, he told Kenny. He had to be on the 2.50 p.m. train this afternoon.

'To York?' Kenny asked hopefully. His dad's job on the trains often took him there and Kenny knew that York had been one of the biggest towns in Roman times. There were all sorts of things he could pick up there to show off in Mrs Clegg's Roman class.

His dad shook his head. He was going off down to Euston, in London, he said, and he couldn't take Kenny. Not this time anyway.

'But you said . . .' Kenny began and his voice trailed off. It seemed that his dad had been breaking more and more of his promises lately. It was almost as if he had some other things on his mind.

His grandad ruffled his hair. 'I'll tell you what – I'll use my railcard and we could go down to Chester,' he suggested brightly. 'There's a great Roman museum there. How about it? I've got all the time in the world . . .'

Kenny didn't say anything, but continued to glare accusingly at his dad.

'I'll take you on my day off,' Mr Bayfield promised.

'And when will that be?' Kenny asked sulkily. 'You don't seem to have many days off these days . . .'

Mr Bayfield took a deep breath, as though he was about to say something important to his son. Then it seemed that he changed his mind at the last moment. He occupied himself by putting the last of the garden tools in the wheelbarrow and wheeling it to the tiny creosote-painted shed which belonged to Grandad Bayfield.

Kenny felt his grandad put his arm on his shoulder. 'C'mon,' he said cheerfully. 'Let's see what old Gran's rustled up – I could eat a horse!'

Kenny didn't say anything, but continued to watch his dad. He was hiding something from him, he was sure of that; and Kenny was determined to find out what.

*

31

Nicky always hated the visiting room at Strangeways prison: row upon row of tiny wooden tables, with the prisoners sat behind them in their blue prison shirts and black trousers, talking to their families. There was no privacy there, because steely-faced prison guards were always on hand – listening to what you had to say; watching you like hawks to make sure that you didn't smuggle anything in. There was no opportunity here to tell your dad what you really felt or just how much you were missing him.

They all missed Billy Power, but none of them really looked forward to visiting days. Every time he, his mum and his older sister Tracey came here they always ended up having arguments with each other, and today had been no exception. Nicky had been late for the bus into Manchester because of his allotment visit, and that had started his mother off. And when Tracey had joined in, their mother had turned on her. She was a fine one to talk, she had said, after having come home at half-past twelve last night, and, no, she didn't believe that she'd been out at Guides until that time!

They were all tense and irritable; after all, none of them liked seeing Billy cooped up in prison like an animal in a cage. But Billy Power had broken the law and been caught, so now he had to serve his time behind bars for as long as it pleased Her Majesty.

Unless, of course, thought Nicky, unless of course my escape plan works!

Billy smiled at his son across the table, thinking how daft Nicky looked in his collar and tie. He'd have much preferred to see him in the T-shirt and jeans he normally wore at home; and he'd rather have seen his wife in the usual clothes she wore around the house than the tight mini-skirt, high heels and tons of make-up she'd put on in an unsuccessful effort to impress him.

'So, how's that new school of yours, son?' he asked.

'It's not so new now,' Mrs Power interrupted before Nicky even had a chance to reply. 'He's been there nearly a year now . . .'

Billy grinned at his wife; a hard, false grin that told her to shut up. He turned back to Nicky. 'You working hard?' he asked. 'You got some mates?'

Nicky shrugged casually, but Mrs Power butted in again. 'Course he has! What about Lee?'

'I'm sick of Lee,' Nicky said sulkily.

'He's just jealous,' piped up Tracey, who had on almost as much make-up as her mother. 'He's jealous cos Lee's dad's moved back in . . .'

Billy ignored Nicky's protests and smiled kindly at his son. They still understood each other, he realized, despite the fact that he was in prison.

'It won't be long till I'm out of here,' he promised Nicky. 'Then you and I can spend some time together.' He pinched Nicky's still scrawny arms. 'We'll be able to do some weights together, and build you up.'

Tracey yawned, and started eyeing up a particularly muscular and handsome prisoner sitting a few tables down the row. Mrs Power wagged a scolding finger at her husband.

'Don't you get him going, Billy!' she chided. 'It could be ages yet!'

Billy shook his head. 'It won't be long before I'm

out,' he said, and winked at Nicky. 'If I don't hear from my solicitor by first thing Monday then we'll put the plan into operation!'

Nicky's eyes shone and he clenched his fist in a triumphant gesture.

Mrs Power urged Nicky to calm down and then scolded her husband once again, telling him to stop teasing Nicky. But Billy continued.

'The helicopter's all booked,' he told Nicky. Tracey lifted her eyes heavenwards, amazed that her younger brother could believe such rubbish. 'It'll hover over the yard . . .'

'Yeah, and you'll run from your exercise,' Nicky continued. He could see it all now in his mind's eye. 'You'll grab hold of the escape ladder . . .'

His dad's eyes twinkled as he carried on with their dream scenario. 'The helicopter drops me off somewhere on the moors . . . There'll be a stash of food waiting for me . . .'

'And a safe hiding-place,' added Nicky. His dad could hide out in the old shack on the allotment until the heat died down, and Scratch was going to be a really great guard dog. If he and his dad worked together on this one, then the police would never track them down!

'Yeah, and I'll lay low,' his dad said, warming to their fantasy. 'And then after a bit, bob's your uncle!'

Mrs Power looked at Nicky. His eyes were shining bright with anticipation. She turned to her husband. 'Stop it, Billy!'

Billy's face fell; he knew she was right, for once. He smiled sadly at Nicky. 'Only joking,' he muttered, and disappointment flooded Nicky's face. 'If only, eh, Nick?'

Nicky bit his lips, but refused to let his dad see just how upset he was. He'd believed his dad when he said that he was going to make a break for it. That's why he'd got the puppy in the first place. It had felt good, planning things with his dad again, just like in the old days before he had got put inside. It only went to show that you should never take at face value anything grown-ups ever say to you.

'Yeah, it was only a joke, wasn't it, Dad?' he said, but there was a quiver in his voice which betrayed him. Suddenly Nicky Power felt very much alone in the world.

Chapter Four

Richard Skellern wheeled his mud-covered bicycle awkwardly down the corridor of Barton Wood. It was Monday morning, and teachers and pupils were rushing to and fro, caught up in the usual start-of-week madness, so no one paid much attention to him.

If they had, they would have seen that he was a good-looking man in his early twenties, with eager, sparkling eyes and his hair tied back in a ponytail. He was dressed in a pair of jeans and a jacket and tie. The jacket and tie fitted him so badly that it was obvious they didn't belong to him. In fact, he had borrowed them from a friend for the day. Richard Skellern was the new student teacher at Barton Wood and he was determined to make a good impression on his first day.

As he looked around the corridor, uncertain which way to turn, he saw Lee and Kenny approaching him. The two boys were deep in conversation and he strained to hear what they were talking about.

'Kerton gave his puppy back to Swainsgate,' Kenny informed Lee. He had been in the school secretary's office handing in a class register when a sheepish Joe had given Stevie back over to her, telling her that things had changed at home and that it would be impossible to keep the pup.

Mrs Swainsgate had agreed to find the dog a new home, after she had shaken her head and told him in no uncertain terms that he should have checked before taking on the responsibility. In the sort of voice she normally used for telling off people who had forgotten to bring in their dinner money, she said that she hadn't thought to ask grown-ups to bring in a note. Joe, feeling about two feet tall, had then slunk off to his office, where he had promised to keep Stevie until Mrs Swainsgate could find him another home.

'That does it,' said Lee when Kenny had told him the news. 'We'll tell Power. If Swainsgate can take one back then she can take two. He'll have to give Scratch back. He can't live in that shed for ever, living on nicked . . .'

He stopped as he noticed Richard Skellern standing in the corridor. He was studying a scrap of paper, and he nodded a welcome to the two boys.

'Hi, lads,' he said breezily, and introduced himself. 'I'm looking for Mrs –' he consulted the piece of paper once again – 'Mrs Sherry.'

'You'll have to wait in the staffroom then,' said Lee after Kenny had told him that she had just gone off to Mr Higgins's class. 'Make yourself a cup of tea in there – that's what they all do.' He pointed to the open door at the far end of the corridor.

Mr Skellern nodded and then looked doubtfully down at his bicycle. 'Will it be safe out here in the corridor?' he asked.

Kenny sighed. Would it be safe in the corridor at Barton Wood? Would pigs fly over Manchester Cathedral?

'No –' he began, but Lee kicked him.

'Yeah, course it'll be safe,' Lee lied. Kenny looked curiously at his mate: what game was he up to now?

Mr Skellern grinned his thanks and followed the

two boys to the empty staffroom, leaving his bike unattended in the corridor. When they had promised to tell Mrs Sherry that he had arrived, and Mr Skellern had closed the staffroom door, Lee scurried over to the young student's bike. He started to wheel it down the corridor, leaving a track of mud and dirt behind him, with Kenny following in hot pursuit.

He stopped at the green door which led to Mrs Sherry's office. With a mischievous grin on his face, he rapped on the door. Satisfied that the headteacher hadn't unexpectedly returned to her office, he opened the door and wheeled the bicycle inside.

'Kerton gave his dog back,' Lee whispered to Esi when he and Kenny had finally arrived in the classroom, late as usual, and much to Mrs Clegg's annoyance.

'Little Norton?' she asked.

'Stevie,' interrupted Miranda, who was walking past their table and had overheard. 'His name is Stevie.' She stormed angrily back to her own place, her heart beating furiously.

So Joe had finally done what he'd said he would. He'd given little Stevie back. He'd let her down. Miranda promised herself she would never forgive Joe for that. Never.

Kenny glanced uneasily over at Nicky, who was sitting by himself, concentrating on drawing up yet another elaborate plan for releasing his dad from prison.

'Someone's got to tell him to give the dog back,' Kenny whispered to Esi.

Esi frowned. 'Why?' she asked.

'I think it was a stupid idea in the first place,' Roberta said snootily. She still hadn't quite forgiven her own parents for not allowing her to have one of the puppies.

'Someone has got to tell him!' Kenny repeated, and slowly everyone's eyes turned on to Lee. Lee gulped as he realized that he'd just been volunteered.

After class Miranda didn't go off to play with the others. Instead she wandered over to Joe's tiny room, looking through the doorway at Stevie, who was lying in a cardboard box in the corner of the room.

All she really wanted to do was to rush in and stroke and cuddle the puppy, but she knew that if she did, then it would be even harder to leave him. That was the trouble with things you loved, she'd found out: sooner or later they were always taken away from you. Like her baby brother, who shared Stevie's name, you couldn't hold on to them.

Joe walked up quietly behind her, and whispered hello. Miranda turned around angrily, refusing to look Joe in the face. She could still see Stevie from out of the corner of her eye.

Joe came round, and knelt down in front of her, forcing her to look him in the eye. 'Miranda, I'm sorry,' he began.

Miranda didn't reply, and just stared angrily at him, making him feel even more guilty.

'I didn't know,' Joe said, referring to the baby. 'You know I wouldn't have let you down and neither would Jackie. You're our friend . . .'

'That's the second Stevie I've lost,' Miranda said simply. Tears began to run down her face.

'You're our very best friend,' Joe repeated.

'Yeah, and I won't be no more, will I!' she burst out. 'You won't want me any more when you've got your baby, will you!'

Once again everyone had let Miranda down; she'd thought Joe and Jackie might have been different from her mum and dad and the teachers at Barton Wood, but they'd proved to be just the same.

But then life was like that, Miranda thought bitterly, and you just learnt to get on with it the best way you could.

Brushing the tears away from her eyes, she set off down the corridor to the infants' class; at least the little kids at Barton Wood needed her, she thought. She'd never let them down like Joe did.

Then she remembered that Joe and Jackie would soon be having a little kid of their own, and her heart softened a little towards the Kertons. Maybe when it was born they'd let her play with the baby and look after it, just like she'd wanted to look after Stevie. At least it was something to hope for.

Joe winked at her and smiled warmly as she walked away. He knew how disappointed Miranda must be, so he resolved there and then that somehow he'd make it up to her. Miranda had to know that there was at least one person in the world who wanted her and loved her.

Jack Higgins gave himself a silent pat on the back as he supervised the playground at break-time. It had been a gamble inviting old Albert Dawson to come and give his class a talk on the mine he'd worked in, which had first opened in Victorian times.

After all, Albert had never spoken in public before, not least of all to a class of twenty-odd seven-year-olds. He was also pushing seventy and had a reputation for absent-mindedness.

However, as soon as the pupils had started asking him questions about his life down the mine, he had relaxed. Soon he was fascinating them with stories of the pit ponies and the child labourers who used to work at Barton Wood colliery. Children as young as Liam and Mandy and the others used to work in the colliery from six o'clock in the morning, he had told them, and Mr Higgins had secretly grinned. Just let Liam moan again about having to be in school by nine o'clock!

He smiled at Richard Skellern, who had finally been discovered in the staffroom by Mrs Sherry and introduced to the deputy head. Not, however, before Mrs Sherry had discovered Mr Skellern's bike parked in her office, and her carpet covered in mud and dirt.

Mrs Sherry had put him on playground duty with Mr Higgins in the hope that the older teacher might give him a valuable lesson in how to protect himself against practical jokes from the likes of Lee and Nicky.

Mr Higgins pointed over to a far corner of the playground. Albert was there now, surrounded by a group of children, playing a game of marbles, or 'dibsies' as he liked to call them. It was as if the old codger had rediscovered his lost youth by being surrounded by young people again.

A little way off from Albert and his new-found friends, and well away from the ears of Mr Higgins and Richard Skellern stood Esi, Kenny and Lee. Esi nodded over to Nicky, who was sitting on a ball in the football area, gloomily studying his sheet of paper.

'Well, are you going to do it or not?' she asked Lee, using the type of voice her mother used when she wanted Esi to tidy her room.

Lee sulked, as Nicky saw them and started to walk over. 'Why me?' he asked miserably.

'Because you're his mate, that's why,' she hissed, and indicated that he should be silent as Nicky came over to join them, carrying the football and the sheet of paper underneath his arm.

Nicky nodded a welcome to Kenny and Esi, and then turned to Lee. 'Shop tonight,' he said, all secretively. 'OK?'

Lee shuffled awkwardly, and looked down at the ground.

'You're not bottling out, are you?' Nicky demanded sharply.

'No, but . . .'

'We think you should give the dog back,' said Kenny. 'It's not fair . . . It's cruel to keep it.'

Nicky still carried on looking at Lee with narrowed, suspicious eyes. 'You haven't told her about you-know-where, have you?' he whispered, indicating Esi.

'No!' Lee replied defensively.

'You'd better not,' Nicky threatened. 'Cos I've got big plans.' He looked menacingly at his friend. 'Shop tonight. OK?'

Lee nodded, as the whistle for the end of breaktime went, and Nicky walked off back to the main school building.

Esi looked despairingly at Lee. 'Well, you really told him, didn't you?' she said sarcastically, and followed Nicky back into school.

Later that evening Kenny's gran was at the checkout in Mr Vasisht's shop, busy ticking off a list of items. Chatting to her at the till was Kompel, one of Kenny's classmates and Mr Vasisht's daughter. Kompel often helped her dad out in the shop in the evenings and at weekends for some extra pocket-money.

By the till there was a TV screen, which was linked to the security cameras around the small store. Kompel hardly ever looked at it, however; she was usually far too busy helping customers like Gran Bayfield, or catching up on her homework at the checkout.

From out of the corner of her eye she saw Nicky enter the shop, carrying a large shoulderbag. Kompel looked long and hard at him, until he pulled a face at her and disappeared behind some shelves.

She turned back to Gran Bayfield and started to add up her grocery bill. Then Lee came into the shop. He looked around nervously and joined Nicky by the baked beans.

'I thought you were going to chicken out again,' Nicky said, and started to take several cans of baked beans from the shelf and drop them into his open bag.

'Dogs don't eat beans!' Lee protested.

'Don't make it so obvious!' Nicky hissed, and told him to keep quiet. 'Now you go and get something. You're in on this dog too, you know!'

'I'm not pinchin' stuff,' Lee stated, and added, 'And it's not fair to keep things locked up!'

Nicky moved on down the aisle and put a tin of rice pudding into his open bag. 'You're right,' he said. 'It ain't fair for things to be locked up. So me and my old man are doing something about it.' He glared at Lee. 'You ain't the only one with a dad, Rayner.'

Lee shook his head again. He knew how much Nicky missed his dad, but that was no excuse for breaking the law. What Nicky was doing was wrong and he was going to have nothing to do with it. He walked away down the aisle and out of the shop.

Nicky shrugged and continued to load his bag with more cans.

What he didn't know was that he was being watched. At the checkout, while Kompel was totalling her bill, Gran Bayfield was watching everything on the closed-circuit TV camera.

Chapter Five

'Someone has been stealing,' Gran announced to Kenny in the kitchen the following morning. Kenny's face went white: had she discovered that he'd nicked the bananas and crumpets the other day for Nicky's dog?

'Nicky, that friend of yours,' his gran added, and Kenny heaved a sigh of relief. 'I saw him taking things from Mr Vasisht's shop . . .'

Kenny became even more worried when Gran explained that she had phoned Mr Vasisht with the news last night. The shopkeeper had told her that he was going to call Mrs Sherry first thing this morning.

'You grassed Nicky up!' he cried.

Didn't his gran understand? You didn't tell tales on your mates, especially someone as mean and hard as Nicky Power. If Nicky found out that it was Kenny's gran who had split on him, then Kenny's life at Barton Wood wouldn't be worth living.

His father came into the kitchen with his grandad. He knew what Kenny was thinking. He smiled encouragingly at him. 'Don't worry, Tiger, if there's any comeback, then they're going to have to answer to me.'

As he struggled into his coat and slung his bag over his shoulder Kenny wasn't so sure. He didn't know if even his dad would be able to protect him from Nicky, especially as he was spending more and more time away from the house, like Saturday when he had gone down to London by himself. Not entirely convinced that he would be returning home alive tonight, Kenny left for school.

After he had gone, Gran sighed. 'I did do the right thing, didn't I?' she asked her husband uncertainly.

'That lad Nicky's done wrong and he has to be punished for it,' Grandad Bayfield replied. Then he looked meaningfully over at Kenny's father. 'And talking of doing the right thing . . .'

'I know,' Mr Bayfield said, in response to the unasked question. 'When am I going to tell Kenny about Sheila?'

'Michael, if you and this lass are getting serious about each other, then you're going to have to be honest with Kenny,' said his father. 'Whether you like it or not!'

'Why's everyone dressed up daft?' Mrs Power asked as she sat near Mrs Swainsgate's office, waiting for her appointment with Mrs Sherry.

Nicky's mother had arrived at Barton Wood about ten minutes ago and, since then, she'd seen almost nobody dressed in normal clothes. Everyone looked, instead, like they were going to a fancy-dress party.

It was like stepping into a time warp to the nineteenth century, she decided, as she settled back into the visitors' chair with a steaming hot cup of coffee. There were girls dressed in long flowing dresses like something out of an episode of a classic TV series, and young boys dressed up as Victorian chimney-sweeps. She'd even seen Mr Higgins striding down the corridor in a long frock-coat and wing-collared shirt, sporting an enormous pair of bushy stick-on sideburns; he'd said he was pretending to be Disraeli-something-or-other, whoever he might be.

She repeated her question loudly to Mrs Swainsgate, who stopped her typing and smiled. Even she looked odd, Mrs Power decided, dressed up like she was in a long black dress and perky little mob-cap.

'We're having a Victorian Day to mark the official opening of the school kitchens,' she explained, leaving Mrs Power none the wiser.

Nicky's mother couldn't see what dressing up in Victorian clothes had to do with school dinners. She sighed disapprovingly: school had never been like this when she was Nicky's age. There was none of this fancy dressing-up then; in her day you had to wear a school uniform and look smart and tidy.

She looked impatiently at her watch. She'd been planning to go round to the hairdressers this morning until she had received that urgent phone call from Mrs Sherry. After reassuring her that Nicky hadn't been involved in any sort of accident, the head had asked her to come around to the school straight away. Well, there'd better be a good reason for it! she'd said to herself.

There was a rap at the door and Nicky walked in to the reception area. His face fell as soon as he laid eyes on his mum. Mrs Power stood up from her chair, knocking over her shopping bags, and crossed over to her son.

'What have you been up to now?' she demanded.

Nicky shrugged. All he knew was that he had been unexpectedly called out of Cleggie's class and told to report directly to the head's office. On the way there he'd been trying to list all the things he might have

47

done wrong in the past week; teasing some of the younger kids in Mr Higgins's class, perhaps. If his mum had been asked to come around though, then it had to be something pretty serious.

Mrs Swainsgate ushered them into the adjoining office. The instant Nicky saw Mr Vasisht sitting next to Mrs Sherry he knew exactly what was up. Suddenly Nicky Power wished he was a hundred thousand miles from Barton Wood. But, even more than that, he wanted to know exactly which scuzzball had grassed on him.

Once Mrs Power and Nicky had sat down on the two chairs in front of her desk, Mrs Sherry explained that certain items had been found missing from Mr Vasisht's shop.

Nicky remained silent, but his mum was outraged. No, more than that, she *exploded*.

'I get it,' she said angrily. 'Like father, like son, yeah? Nicky's dad is in prison for thieving, so that means that Nicky *must* have done it!' She looked across to her son, who was staring at his feet as he swung them to and fro. He was still saying nothing.

Mr Vasisht harrumphed. 'One of my customers says she saw your boy putting things into his bag,' he said softly.

Mrs Sherry ignored Mrs Power and looked at Nicky. 'Did you take things from Mr Vasisht's shop without paying?' she asked him.

'Go on, say you never done it!' said Mrs Power, and prodded Nicky, who still remained silent. As far as Mrs Sherry was concerned, that silence was as good an admission of guilt as anything; but Mrs Power still didn't want to believe that her only son was following in his dad's criminal footsteps.

'How many kids nick from your shop every day?' she asked Mr Vasisht. 'Plenty, I reckon.'

She sighed, finally forcing herself to face the truth.

Mr Vasisht smiled kindly; he had children of his own, he told her, and if the school could sort out the matter, then he promised that he wouldn't involve the police.

'I suppose I should be grateful . . .' Mrs Power said, trying to preserve what little dignity she had left.

Just you wait till you get home tonight, Nicky Power! she thought angrily. Then I'll teach you a lesson you're not going to forget in a hurry!

Mrs Sherry continued to look at Nicky, who still refused to look up and meet her eyes.

'I think you'd better apologize to Mr Vasisht and promise him that it won't happen again,' she said.

'I'm-sorry-it-won't-happen-again.' Nicky mumbled his half-hearted apology.

Mr Vasisht then turned to Mrs Power.

'I'm afraid I must ask you to pay for the dog food and biscuits that Nicky took,' he began.

Nicky finally raised his head. There was a look of alarm on his face. Now he was *really* in for it!

'Dog food?' Mrs Power was confused. 'We ain't got no dog!'

Mrs Sherry was even more confused. 'But what about Mrs Swainsgate's puppy?' she asked. 'You sent in a note . . .'

All eyes suddenly turned on to Nicky, who was wishing that the ground would open up and swallow him. His mother gave him a look which seemed to say: OK, I'm waiting – and there had better be a good explanation!

49

'I typed out a permission note and said it was from you,' Nicky confessed to his mother, 'so that I could have a dog.'

For once Mrs Power was speechless. She could hardly believe what she was hearing. One crook was bad enough in the family, but now Nicky was turning out to be not just a thief, but a forger as well!

Mrs Sherry stood up, sighing, and led Mr Vasisht out of the office, promising that he would be reimbursed for the things Nicky had stolen. She asked Nicky to wait outside while she had a chat with his mother.

As soon as she had closed the door, Mrs Power looked the head straight in the eye. 'Go on – say it,' she said miserably. '"We don't want him growing up like his father . . ."'

'Well, do you?' Mrs Sherry asked.

Mrs Power shook her head sadly. 'He's not a bad lad, you know . . .'

Mrs Sherry smiled kindly. 'I know he's not,' she said. 'So let's try and keep it that way, shall we?'

Mrs Power nodded her thanks and left the office, where Nicky was waiting for her outside. As soon as they were out of Mrs Sherry's sight she gave Nicky an evil-looking stare which made him realize that he was in really big trouble this time.

'Let's see what your father has to say about this!' she said, and stormed off down the corridor. Nicky followed behind, wondering whether to tell her that it was because he had wanted to help his father that he had got into this trouble in the first place.

After they had left, Mrs Sherry shut the door behind them and breathed a long sigh of relief. She had had a feeling this morning that today was not going to be an easy one at Barton Wood. She looked down at her watch. It wasn't even ten o'clock yet and already she'd had to deal with one case of shoplifting, and another of fraud. Now all that she had left to do was sort out what was going to happen to Nicky's dog.

Well, Mrs Swainsgate could deal with that little problem, she decided; after all, if the school secretary had taken the trouble to study Nicky's note more carefully in the first place, then none of this would have happened.

Mrs Sherry sighed again, an even longer and more drawn out one this time. Sometimes it seemed like she was running a home for wayward dogs and trainee master-criminals, and not a school at all!

Back in Mrs Clegg's class everyone was busy making papier mâché helmets and other pieces of 'armour' for the 'Roman' dummy that Mrs Clegg had brought in. Richard Skellern, who was helping out in the class today, busied himself moving from table to table offering encouragement and assistance wherever it was needed.

Watching from her desk Mrs Clegg remarked that the people who seemed to need the most help from Mr Skellern were the girls. Lyn and Esi, especially, giggled each time he approached them. She reminded herself to have a friendly word with him later: if he wasn't careful the girls' crush on him could get out of hand.

What had already seemed to have got out of hand was Lee's wild idea that the ghosts of Roman soldiers could be seen all around the grounds of Barton Wood. It was only a mischievous joke on his part, she knew, but if any of the younger children got to hear about it, she foresaw some tear-stained and worried faces. She promised herself a word to Lee about that too, in private, and then realized that she seemed to be having 'words' with lots of people these days. That was the trouble with being one of the older teachers on the school staff: you thought you'd seen it all and that you were duty-bound to offer everyone the benefit of your experience.

She was pleased, though, that all the pupils in her class seemed to be enjoying their Roman project. Everyone except one, that was. Kenny Bayfield was staring into space, showing not the slightest interest in either the helmet he was making or even his friend Lee's spooky tales of Roman ghosts and demons that haunted the school.

Little did Mrs Clegg know that Kenny would have been quite happy to meet a Roman ghost right now: he wouldn't even have minded meeting a whole army of them. Anything would have been preferable to all the tortures he imagined Nicky Power had in store for him when he realized that it was Kenny's own gran who had shopped him to Mr Vasisht and Mrs Sherry!

Chapter Six

Dressed up in 'Victorian' rags, Joe Kerton felt a right idiot. Even though he wasn't part of the teaching staff, Joe always liked to get into the spirit of things. So, along with everyone else, he'd dressed up for the Victorian Day. It hadn't half given Jackie some laughs too.

It was OK, though, because everyone else was doing the same thing at school. What Joe hadn't expected was being asked by Mrs Swainsgate to track down Nicky's puppy on the allotments. That had meant a walk down the main street in his rags, and he had attracted more than his fair share of strange looks and sniggers.

He looked down the rows of allotment sheds, wondering which one Scratch was in. A few gardeners and vegetable-growers stared curiously at him, wondering who this funny-looking tramp was. A couple even asked themselves if they should call the police or not.

Fortunately most of them recognized Joe and thought it better to ask him why he was dressed in old rags; weren't they paying him enough at that new school where he was working?

Finally Joe heard a muffled bark from one of the most decrepit-looking shacks, and rushed over. The mud splashed against his trousers, making his tramp costume look even more lifelike.

He creaked open the flimsy wooden door to the

shed, and Scratch yapped in welcome. Scratch was lying on an old sleeping-bag and, as Joe entered the shack, he came bounding towards him, wagging his tail behind him. Joe grinned and scooped him up in his arms.

'OK, pal,' he said cheerfully, 'I'm taking you back to civilization – well, Barton Wood at least!'

'What the blue blazes d'yer think you're doing in my shed!' barked a gruff and threatening voice from behind him.

Joe spun round, but relaxed when he recognized Albert, the old codger who had given Mr Higgins's class a talk on the Barton Wood colliery, and who had also started the school's new craze for playing marbles.

'I thought you were one of them squatters,' Albert explained as he recognized Joe. He nodded down at Scratch, who was nestling comfortably in Joe's arms. 'Who's yer friend?'

Joe told him the story of Nicky getting the dog without permission and how Mrs Swainsgate had asked him to find the dog and return him to her. When Albert heard that Scratch needed a new owner his old eyes lit up. He came over and stroked the dog.

'I've had dogs all me life,' he said. 'I wouldn't mind looking after this little beauty . . .'

Joe had been lucky when he'd returned Stevie to Mrs Swainsgate: old Mrs Tarbuck, a friend of hers from the church, had wanted to take him on. But as far as he knew there was no one else who wanted a pup.

'You'll need to ask Olive Swainsgate about that,'

he said. 'Why not come back with me now?' he suggested. 'They're about to hold the official opening of the school kitchens.' He winked. 'You never know, you might be able to talk yourself into a free feed!'

'You're on!'

Back at Barton Wood Mr Higgins had put the whole of the teaching staff on Bamber alert. Dressed in an ill-fitting Victorian teacher's frock-coat and waistcoat, which gaped wide-open over his sizeable stomach, Councillor Bamber was flitting around the playground with a camcorder in his hand. He was recording Mr Higgins's class in their Victorian costumes as they played dibsies, cheering them on whenever anyone played a particularly good shot.

Finally he decided that he wanted to get into the action himself, and asked around to see if anyone could operate a camcorder. Paul Haines, who had been standing a little way off watching the game, put up his hand – his dad used one at home for home videos – and Mr Bamber handed the camcorder over to him.

Mr Bamber stroked his chin thoughtfully. 'Let's stage a right bit of proper Victorian schoolstuff for the camera,' he suggested with an enthusiasm which wasn't exactly matched by the others.

He drew out a long wicker cane from his belt, then sliced it through the air with a swishing sound which made everyone jump back.

'If the pupils were naughty they used to get six of the best with this!' Len Bamber announced, and laughed like a mad Victorian schoolmaster. Kenny and the others, who had come to see what all the fuss was about, giggled gleefully.

Mr Bamber strode towards Kenny, who pretended to cringe with fear, as the cane came swishing down in his direction. The others screamed with delight as Mr Bamber pretended to beat Kenny with the cane.

'That's for breathing!' he yelled, starting to get into his role as the evil teacher. He swiped at Kenny with the cane again. 'And that's for wearing trainers!'

'Please, sir, don't beat me again!' yelled Kenny, enjoying the play-acting. 'I'm still hurting from the last time!'

Bamber laughed even more loudly, and brought the cane down in Kenny's direction again.

Suddenly everyone fell silent.

Bamber halted his arm in mid-air, and looked across to where everyone was pointing. He gulped. An Oriental-looking man and woman and a young girl were staring at him in horror. The girl had buried her face in the man's side and was sobbing.

Len Bamber hastily lowered his cane. He realized the impression he must have made on the three strangers. They didn't stay around to hear his explanation. Instead they turned away hurriedly and quickly marched across the playground to the main entrance. Mr Bamber ran after the three terrified newcomers, but this made them walk even faster. Behind him, Kenny and Paul and the others howled with laughter.

'Wait. I think I ought to explain,' he cried as he finally caught up with them in the corridor which led to Mrs Sherry's office. The man turned around and smiled at Mr Bamber, all the time keeping a wary eye on the cane that the councillor was still holding in his hand.

'I'm one of the school governors,' Len Bamber

began, and waved the cane in the air. 'I wasn't really caning those kids . . . I mean I'd never . . .'

'It's obvious that Barton Wood is having a special day,' the man said pleasantly enough. Bamber noticed that the young girl didn't seem quite so sure, and kept very close to the woman's side.

Mrs Sherry smiled; she'd seen the whole thing and knew exactly what Mr and Mrs Lung and their daughter Kim must have thought. 'I'd give up while you're ahead, Councillor Bamber,' she said, trying hard not to laugh.

'I was just . . . you might think . . . well, I . . .'

'Why don't you go back to the playground?' Mrs Sherry suggested sweetly. He could do the least damage there.

Mr Bamber took up the suggestion a little too eagerly and turned and raced back down the corridor and away from this highly embarrassing situation. As the amused Mrs Sherry watched him go she wondered how she was going to convince shy young Kim, the newest pupil at Barton Wood, that not all the adults at the school where quite as weird as Councillor Bamber.

Although, thinking of Joe Kerton, Olive Swainsgate with her dogs, and Jack Higgins dressed like Prime Minister Disraeli from the nineteenth century, she wasn't so sure . . .

It was almost dinnertime, and a buzz of excitement ran through the school as Mrs Clegg's class helped Joe, Albert and Richard Skellern move desks and chairs to prepare the hall for dinner. The official opening of the kitchens was considered to be so important that even a photographer from the *Irwell Valley Recorder* had been invited to cover the event.

The door to the hall opened and Mrs Sherry walked in. There was a gasp of astonishment from the waiting children. Mrs Sherry was dressed in a long, full, black gown with a bustle, and on her head she wore a white bonnet, while there was a purplish sash across her chest. Very few people could believe that the royal-looking person in their midst was in fact their headteacher.

Miranda was stunned. 'Wow, miss, you look like a queen!'

Mrs Sherry gave Miranda a royal wave of her hand. 'Queen Victoria, to be precise,' she said. She turned to Mrs Clegg, who was also dressed in Victorian costume, although nothing as impressive as hers. 'Do I look as silly as I feel?' she asked anxiously.

'You look marvellous,' Mrs Clegg reassured her as Councillor Bamber came into the hall, still dressed in his schoolmaster's outfit.

He bowed before Mrs Sherry. 'Your Majesty!' he cried, and kissed Mrs Sherry's hand. Behind him Lee and Nicky started to chuckle. It was true what they had always suspected: when it came to being daft, you couldn't beat grown-ups!

Mrs Sherry seemed to agree with them. She looked over nervously at the group of dinner ladies who were impatiently waiting for the school kitchens to be officially declared open. Unlike everyone else they were dressed in the blue uniforms which they wore every day. Sighing, she urged Councillor Bamber to cut the blue tape across the kitchen door and declare the kitchen open.

'And now for our special Victorian lunch,' she said, after Bamber had cut the tape. 'Our main course was a big hit for the Victorians – fish and chips!' A cheer went up. 'But before that there's the first course,' she said, as dinner ladies started bringing in steaming bowls of soup on trays. 'Soup made by boiling old meat bones!'

The cheer turned into a howl of dismay. Miranda looked down suspiciously at her bowl and sniffed it. She made a face and looked up at Mrs Sherry.

'Miss, it smells like cat-pee . . .'

Mrs Sherry sighed.

Chapter Seven

In the prison waiting-room Billy Power looked up as his wife and Nicky made their way to his table. This was their second visit to him in four days, and it was a school day, he realized, which could mean only one thing: there was trouble at home.

Mrs Power sat down at his table and wasted no time in getting to the point. She nodded over at Nicky. 'He's been caught lifting biscuits and dog-food!' she said.

Billy couldn't help but laugh: he didn't even know that they had a dog. 'So Nick's been nicking, eh?' he said, and laughed at his own joke, until a warning look from Mrs Power made him shut up.

'I was doing it for you, Dad,' Nicky protested. 'I'd got you a hiding-place and a guard dog.'

He looked around to make sure that none of the screws, as his dad called them, were listening. 'It was for your escape,' he said, perfectly serious. 'Y'know, in the helicopter . . .'

Billy threw back his head and roared with laughter. Nicky frowned. Why was his dad laughing so much, after they'd talked such a lot about his escape plan?

'You thought your dad could escape, you little fool?' his mum asked, and then turned angrily on Billy, who was still laughing. 'See! He believes every word you say! Just like I did once! He thinks you're a hero!'

'He is, Mum,' Nicky said.

'*He is not!*' she said. There was anger in her voice. It was difficult to tell whether it was anger at herself for marrying Billy in the first place, at Billy for telling Nicky wild stories, or at Nicky for believing them.

'Tell Nicky what it's really like in prison, Billy,' she said. 'Tell him about being locked in a cell for twenty-three hours of the day. How you can't see any of your mates, or do anything you want to! Do you want Nicky to end up in here, too, Billy?'

Nicky looked from his mother to his father. From the look in his dad's eyes it was obvious that his mum had hit a raw nerve. Billy was staring wistfully in the distance, as if he was trying to see through the stone walls that kept him a prisoner in here. Finally he turned to Nicky.

'The worst is Saturdays and Sundays,' he said softly. 'The outdoor market next to the prison is in full swing then. You can't see it from my cell window, but you can hear it. You can hear people laughing, you can smell onions and hot dogs cooking … I really fancy going down there, having a laugh, getting out in the sun.' He shuddered. 'Sunlight's the one thing you don't see in here …' he said sadly. 'And I'm in here because I've been stupid.'

Nicky shook his head loyally. 'You're the best, Dad,' he said.

Billy looked Nicky right in the eyes. 'If you grew up like me, Nicky … I'd be ashamed of you …'

Nicky found it difficult to speak. All his life he'd hero-worshipped his dad. Every single day he had tried to be a little bit more like him. And now here he was, saying what a mess he'd made of his life.

'Go home,' Billy said. 'And do what your mam tells you to do from now on – or else.'

Nicky wanted to cry, but he didn't. There was no way he was going to let his dad or his mum, or the other cons in the visiting room, see just how upset he was. He pushed his chair back roughly, stood up, and rushed away towards the door. Mrs Power nodded a sad thanks to her husband and then followed her son out of the prison.

Nicky had come in here believing his dad to be a great hero, his best mate. He'd imagined the great times they would have together just as soon as he cracked his way out of the nick. And now he realized that they were nothing more than a bunch of stupid dreams. Nicky was leaving the prison with all his hopes shattered. He felt totally betrayed.

The bell for the end of school sounded and there was a general stampede towards the door. All anyone seemed to want to do was to get home for tea and today's episode of *Neighbours*. Only Nicky slouched along the corridor, seemingly lost in his own little world, and clearly very upset.

Mrs Sherry, still dressed in her Victorian costume, came quietly up to him. She knew that Nicky had been to see his father; she was surprised that he'd bothered to turn up for the afternoon's lessons.

'Is everything all right?' she asked softly.

Nicky looked up at her, and shook his head sulkily.

'Was your father angry?'

Nicky nodded.

'Do you want to talk about it?'

A shake of the head.

Mrs Sherry bent down slightly, to look Nicky in the eye.

'You're not a bad lad, Nicky,' she began kindly. 'And I know it hasn't been easy for you with your dad not at home . . .'

Nicky turned away from her awkwardly and bit his lip. He hadn't cried in front of his dad. And there was no way he was going to cry in front of Mrs Sherry either.

'I hate him!' he cried out with feeling. 'I hate him!'

And with that, Nicky ran off down the corridor. It was only when he knew for certain that no one was spying on him that, at long last, he allowed his tears to fall.

Kenny licked his lips as he continued colouring in the Roman map of Barton Wood that he'd been working on. A pack of coloured crayons was open on the living-room table, and his dad watched on proudly as he worked.

'Everything OK at school today?' he asked, by way of beginning a conversation. Kenny nodded but didn't look up. If he had done he would have noticed that his gran and grandad had left the room. They'd realized that his dad wanted a private chat with him.

Mr Bayfield took a deep breath. Well, now's as good a time as any to tell him, he told himself sternly.

'I'm going to invite a friend around for a meal tomorrow,' he said.

'OK,' said Kenny, and started colouring the Roman villa he had drawn, a bright, sunshiny yellow. 'Does he work on the trains with you?'

'It's not a "he", Kenny, it's a "she" . . .'

Kenny stopped colouring, and looked inquiringly up at his dad. Mr Bayfield had gone red in the face: he was obviously finding this very difficult.

'She's called Sheila. I know you'll like her – she's really nice . . .'

Kenny put his crayon down. 'Is she your girl-friend?' he asked coolly. When his father nodded, he demanded, 'And why haven't you told me about her before?'

'I was worried how you'd feel,' he said.

'Are you going to marry her?'

His dad smiled. 'Kenny, we've only known each other a little while . . .'

'I don't want another mum!' Kenny shouted, and leapt up out of his chair. 'So I don't want your stupid girlfriend in our house.'

Kenny rushed past his dad and his gran, who was just bringing in tea on a tray, and raced upstairs to his room. He slammed the door shut behind him, and threw himself on the bed, sobbing into his pillow.

Chapter Eight

After returned puppies, forged letters, attempted jail-breaks and rumours of ghosts on the school grounds, Mrs Sherry arrived at school the following day, hoping that the next few days might be a little more peaceful.

She should have known better. For a start, the school was back on Bamber alert – the Councillor was due to make one of his regular inspections. Mrs Sherry prayed that he'd be dressed in his normal clothes; it had been quite a job to calm Kim Lung down after he'd scared the life out of her yesterday.

Secondly, no sooner had she entered the main gates of Barton Wood at twenty-past eight than Lyn and Esi came running after her. They had discovered something really dire out on the sports field, they told her, and she had to come and see at once.

Reluctantly she allowed herself to be dragged off to a spot just behind the football pitch goalposts. A small group had already gathered there, including Paul, Kenny, Roberta and Lee.

Mrs Sherry recognized the spot immediately. It was the place where, last term, they had buried a 'time capsule' containing everyday items from Barton Wood village in the 1990s. It was supposed to have been dug up again sometime in the next century. During the night, however, or early this morning, someone had obviously been trying to steal the chest. They had dug a hole in an attempt to pull the chest out of the ground.

Mrs Sherry cleared a way through the onlookers and called Joe Kerton over. Together they heaved the chest out of the hole which had been dug around it.

'This was supposed to be dug up in a hundred years,' she grunted. 'Not every couple of weeks.'

'It wasn't me this time, miss,' Esi protested, remembering the time when she had mislaid her Ghanaian christening headscarf in the chest, and had had to dig up the chest again to retrieve it.

'No one said it was, Esi,' Mrs Sherry smiled, and opened the chest. She knelt down and started to examine its contents. Everything seemed to be in order. Nothing had gone missing.

'Perhaps we surprised 'em?' suggested Joe, and looked around at the nearby bushes and trees as if there might be someone hiding in them. Nobody.

Esi urgently rummaged among the contents of the chest, searching for the Roman coin that they had also left in there. Of course, it wasn't modern, but it had been dug up in the fields when Barton Wood school was being built last year. Everyone had decided to put it in the chest to prove to people in the twenty-first century that Romans had once lived in the area.

'It's down here,' said Paul, shoving his hand down the side of the chest and pulling out the small copper coin. He handed it to Esi.

Mrs Sherry stood up and brushed the dirt and mud from her smart skirt. She shook her head sadly: it seemed that you couldn't trust anyone these days. But what would vandals have wanted with the time capsule? There was nothing particularly valuable in it, after all. She turned to Joe.

'Can you fence this off?' she asked him. 'We'll have to rebury the chest.'

Joe nodded and promised to stand guard on the chest until the police arrived. This was, after all, a case of attempted theft and vandalism, not to mention trespassing on school property, and the Law would have to be called in.

By his side, Esi shivered. She looked down at the Roman coin which she was still clutching tightly in her hand. She suddenly knew exactly who had tried to unearth the time capsule. And she knew that the police were going to be no help whatsoever when it came to tracking down *this* would-be thief.

'I know who did it,' she said, trembling. 'It's that Roman ghost. He's come back. He's come back to get his money . . .'

Mrs Sherry looked at Esi as if to say, Don't be so stupid! There are no such things as ghosts! But several of those there, including Kenny and Joe Kerton himself, weren't quite so sure . . .

'So if any of you older ones know anything about youths or vandals on our field out of school hours, then I want to know about it!' Mrs Sherry announced as she addressed morning assembly half an hour after the discovery on the sports field.

Several people shifted uncomfortably. Esi turned to Lyn and mouthed the word 'ghost'. Esi knew that Mrs Sherry wouldn't find the culprit here in the hall: she'd have a much better chance down at the local graveyard!

Drawing assembly to a close Mrs Sherry lifted up a copy of the *Irwell Valley Recorder*, the local newspaper.

'I want to remind you all about the *Recorder*'s short-story competition for local schools.'

At the back of the hall Lee sighed. How could they forget about it? There were posters advertising it all over the school, for Heaven's sake! And Cleggie had been going on about it like it was the most important thing ever to hit Barton Wood.

'Entries have to be in by tomorrow, so this is your last chance!' Mrs Sherry said. 'I expect many of you have been busy . . .'

She looked out hopefully at her audience. Several people shook their heads; some turned guiltily away. Only Roberta and a few others nodded.

Not to be discouraged, Mrs Sherry continued. 'But it's never too late. You can write about anything in the world, as long as it's fiction – and as long as it's your own work. And the best story will win £500 for the school!'

The infants at the front of the hall nearest Mrs Sherry whooped. Mrs Sherry smiled indulgently: at least they were excited. Which was more than she could say for Nicky Power, who was shaking his head, clearly unimpressed.

'I've brought mine in already,' Roberta announced rather smugly. By her side, Lyn said that she'd nearly finished hers as well.

'And I'm ace at writing stories!' Esi bragged, determined not to be outdone by her two friends.

Mrs Sherry smiled smugly. Let Nicky and Lee be unimpressed, she thought. At least some of their year were getting into the spirit of things.

'You see, everyone's got a story to tell,' she continued. 'It doesn't have to be about kings and queens, or dragons, or space invaders –'

'No, miss!' agreed Lyn. 'It can be about ghosts as well!'

Mrs Sherry exchanged a defeated look with Mrs Clegg, who was sitting at the piano. They were going to have to find out soon who had tried to dig up the time capsule. Or they would have to learn to cope with Barton Wood's reputation for Roman ghosts!

Mrs Sherry wondered whether she ought to ask Years Five and Six to stay behind and tell them about the forthcoming school trip to nearby Boddington Hall.

Finally she decided against it: what with vandals and so-called ghosts everyone had probably had enough excitement for one morning. She would go round the individual classes and tell them later. It was important that anyone who wanted to go on the school trip brought permission letters from their parents. Although, remembering the incident with Nicky and the puppy, she decided that she had better check the letters herself this time, rather than leave the task to Mrs Swainsgate.

Mrs Sherry called an end to assembly, and everyone started to file out of the hall to go off to their classes. As Mr Higgins followed his class out he noticed the tiny figure of Kim Lung standing outside in the corridor.

She was holding a large plastic carrier-bag on which were printed the words 'The Golden Dragon Restaurant'. Mr Higgins was certain that she hadn't been in the hall.

He went up to her and looked pointedly at his watch. 'How long have you been waiting out here, Kim?' he asked.

The Vietnamese girl lowered her head so that she wouldn't have to meet her teacher's gaze. She'd overslept and had just arrived, she admitted, even though it was turning half-past nine. And yes, she knew it wasn't a good start to her second day, and no, she told Mr Higgins, she hadn't brought a note either.

'I'll need a note,' Mr Higgins told her sternly. 'Otherwise it's what's called an "unauthorized absence", and you'll be counted as a truant.'

When Kim didn't reply, he tried another approach and softened the tone of his voice. 'Were you up late last night watching telly?'

Kim shook her head, and Mr Higgins hurried her along to his class. He was worried about Kim already. If she couldn't even start off by getting in to school on time, then she was soon going to be in serious trouble.

Although Barton Wood's Victorian Day had now come and gone, and everyone had enjoyed themselves, Mr Higgins's Victorian project still continued. The Victorian Day had had its desired effect, he realized, as he watched his class working. Everyone was now approaching their tasks with much more interest and enthusiasm.

Mr Higgins clapped his hands to get his class's attention. A few carried on with their work; most looked up, hoping that he might have decided to let them off a little earlier than usual. A couple of them noticed that Mr Higgins looked a little embarrassed – as if he had something important to say but didn't quite know how to start.

'I want to talk to you about Mandy,' he said to the

entire class. Kate looked around: the girl in the wheelchair wasn't in the room. For a second she thought she might have gone off to the disabled toilets, until Sally spoke up and said that she'd gone off to see her physiotherapist.

'I want a word with you all while she's *not* here,' he continued, and when Liam offered to tell Mandy afterwards he had added sharply, 'I don't want you to tell her anything.'

Twenty-five curious faces looked up at him.

'I want you to do what's needed!'

The penny dropped. Most of the class liked Mandy and felt sorry for the fact that she was in a wheelchair. Everyone tried to help her, to make her life easier at Barton Wood.

'You want us to be more kind to her?' asked Kate.

Mr Higgins shook his head. 'No. I want you to be *less* kind!'

Twenty-five puzzled faces looked at each other. What was Mr Higgins going on about?

'You're all over her at the moment,' he told them. 'You're all being ever so nice – opening doors for her, carrying her work around, getting her what she needs.'

Twenty-five faces looked even more confused: wasn't that what they were supposed to do?

'Mandy's got to be independent in her wheelchair,' Mr Higgins said. 'She had more independence before, when she was at her special school. She's come here to Barton Wood to be –' He searched around for the right word, until Arjun found it for him.

'Normal,' Arjun said. 'Normal, like us!'

'That's right. Give her room, and let her fend for

herself,' Mr Higgins said. 'That's how you can all be the most helpful to her.'

Darren leaned back in his chair and whistled in amazement. This was a real turn-up for the books, he thought. A teacher telling them *not* to be too kind or nice to someone!

Today was getting decidedly worse and worse, Mrs Sherry thought, and it was still only the mid-morning break! She stepped through the door into the staff-room to find about twenty huge cardboard boxes blocking her way. For a moment she had a ghastly vision that each of them contained even more litters of yapping puppies. But when she peered into one of them she discovered that they contained toilet-rolls – hundreds and hundreds of toilet-rolls.

She looked behind her to see yet another huge box of toilet-rolls. This one, however, seemed to be on legs. Joe Kerton put down the box he was carrying and grinned sheepishly at Mrs Sherry. Behind him there was another cardboard box on legs; but this pair belonged to Lee Rayner, who was helping Joe out.

'Can I put a couple more in here?' asked Joe. 'There's not enough room to turn around in my office!'

Mrs Sherry examined the requisition note on one of the boxes. It seemed that all of them had been ordered by Mr Dunphy, the previous caretaker. She'd heard of being prepared for an emergency, but this was ridiculous.

Well, there was no contest: they would all have to go back. There was no way she could afford this amount of toilet-rolls on Barton Wood's budget. She had enough trouble finding the funds to keep the school in pencils and rulers, let alone enough toilet-paper to last them all the way to the year 2010!

As Joe and Lee carried even more boxes into the staffroom, Mrs Sherry spied Councillor Bamber for the first time. What with all the rumours of ghosts, not to mention this latest unpleasant surprise, she'd forgotten that today was a Bamber Day.

'Send the whole lot back!' Bamber declared.

He made it sound as if it was the easiest thing in the world, Mrs Sherry thought. Len Bamber might be a school governor and a councillor, but he'd obviously never had to deal with the Local Education Authority. They could take weeks just to send some-one round to see what the matter was.

'Issue 'em all with nappies!' was his great idea. 'It'll save all this aggravation and save the school a whole packet of money!'

'Nappies!' cried Joe, with a longing look in his eyes. He thudded another box down on the staff-room table, knocking over a pile of exercise books Mrs Clegg was intending to mark. 'Have you seen the new ones? They fit right in the palm of your hand . . .'

Mrs Sherry looked suspiciously at Joe. She'd always said that Joe was a big softy; but even she was surprised by his sudden interest in baby clothes. And then the smile of delight on Joe's face told her everything she needed to know.

'Mr Kerton! You clever old thing!'

Joe grinned from ear to ear like a big Cheshire cat. His and Jackie's secret was out now, and he was really glad. Mrs Sherry and Len Bamber came around to congratulate him.

Unnoticed by any of them, Lee put down the box he was carrying and raced off down the corridor to find his mates. There was nothing he liked better than a bit of gossip about one of the teachers. OK, Joe wasn't exactly a teacher, but this piece of news was too good not to pass around. Wait until he told the others about this!

Chapter Nine

'There are no such things as ghosts!'

Mrs Clegg threw her chalk down on to her desk, not out of anger, but out of exasperation. She had been patiently explaining the Roman system of counting, and was even succeeding in getting Miranda interested, when Esi had mentioned the Roman ghost again.

Of course, that had started Lyn off, and then even Paul – who she always considered to be reasonably level-headed – had asked her what she would do if the ghost of the Roman soldier had walked through the door at that moment. It was time to stop this nonsense once and for all, she decided.

'There are no such things as ghosts,' she repeated. 'And even if there were they wouldn't be harmful. A Roman soldier who came back to the place where he'd spent hard years on duty would only do so for a very good reason.' She searched around for an example. 'They often married local women so perhaps he had a girlfriend here . . .'

'Or he came back for his money,' said Lyn.

'We saw where he'd dug down and opened the chest looking for his money,' Esi said, and shivered: suddenly the classroom seemed much colder.

'That was the work of petty vandals,' Mrs Clegg said sternly, and then looked at the dummy of the Roman centurion in the far corner of the room. Dressed in his papier mâché helmet and breastplate and armour, he looked almost lifelike. '*Our* Roman is a much nobler being: a fine young soldier of the line, tall and fine, and fighting fit . . .'

Esi nudged Lyn. 'See! She does believe in him really!'

Mrs Clegg halted her flight of fantasy. If she wasn't careful she was going to get carried away with Esi's stories just like all the others. Fortunately for her the door opened, and Lee came walking into the class. There was a big grin on his face.

Mrs Clegg looked at her watch. It was almost time for lunch and Lee had been missing ever since break. Before she could tell him off he turned to the rest of the class.

'Mr Kerton's wife's having a baby!' he announced.

The entire class erupted into cheers. Some of them were genuinely happy for Joe; even more were glad at the excuse to disrupt the lesson. Even Mrs Clegg allowed herself a little smile.

The only person who wasn't smiling was Miranda, who leapt to her feet.

'I knew that days ago!' she said, angry now that everyone knew her and Joe's little secret. 'It was me who knew first, because he told me first!'

Mrs Clegg tried to make everybody promise not to go blabbing the news around the rest of the school, pointing out that Joe might still want to keep his news a secret.

But deep down she knew that nothing could ever remain secret for long in a place like Barton Wood. She guessed correctly that as soon as the lunch-bell rang Lyn would go straight to her brother Liam's class and spread the news there. By tonight she wouldn't be surprised if the news wasn't common knowledge from Barton Wood to Manchester city centre.

And who could tell? Talking about Joe's baby might even take their minds off that blessed ghost once and for all!

Miranda glared at Joe as he carried a box of toilet-paper across the playground. All around him Lyn, Lee and all the others were congratulating him on his new baby, before running off in their game of tag. As Mrs Clegg had guessed, the news seemed to have shot around the school in the space of ten minutes.

'You said it was our secret, until Jackie got fat,' Miranda reminded him when he came up to her. 'You told me that *I* could tell everyone!'

Joe sighed. Miranda was feeling touchy and who could blame her? Still, it wasn't his fault that his secret had slipped out and Lee had broadcast it to the entire school, was it?

'I'm still going to be its only auntie, aren't I?' Miranda asked hopefully.

'We mustn't have favourites ...' he began. 'But you'll take it for walks, and change its nappy, and cuddle it off to sleep ...'

Miranda smiled dreamily. She loved caring for young children, and animals, but she'd never had to look after a real-life baby before. Well, not since Stevie, anyway ...

'And only me?' she asked solemnly. Joe nodded, and was about to say something else when Lyn ran up to him again.

'Don't forget ...' she reminded him, before being

77

chased after by one of the younger boys. 'Auntie Lyn! You promised me I can be Auntie Lyn!'

Joe could have kicked himself. He looked down at Miranda, realizing just how disappointed she must be feeling right now. She was staring hatefully at Lyn. Joe somehow knew that Miranda and Lyn wouldn't be friends again for a very long time . . .

Esi looked despairingly at her bedroom clock and then at the blank piece of paper in front of her. It was six o'clock. She'd been sitting at her desk for almost half an hour now, and still she hadn't come up with a single idea for a story. Her mind was completely empty. She was great at composition in class, but now, when it really mattered: nothing, one big zero!

She wished she hadn't bragged about just how ace she was at composition. That meant that she had to come up with the goods by tomorrow morning, otherwise Roberta and Lyn would get all the glory in the short-story competition, and she'd end up the laughing stock of the entire school.

There was a tap at the door and her dad came in, bringing with him a mug of steaming-hot tea.

'How's it going?' he asked.

Esi shrugged. 'All right,' she lied.

Mr Mensah smiled and looked down at her blank piece of paper. Esi tapped the side of her head.

'It's all up here,' she said.

'Aha! Working it out comes first,' he said. 'Then you can write it down. I used to write all sorts of stories myself, for my mummy and daddy. You don't need a pen to write – just a nice room to work in, and ideas, and the right frame of mind.'

Ideas! Esi groaned to herself. That's just what I need! And that's exactly what I haven't got!

'She's coming at seven,' Kenny's gran announced as she opened the door to his bedroom. Kenny was lying on his bed, like he'd been for the last couple of hours, still wearing the clothes he had worn today at school. He didn't turn around when Gran walked over to his bed.

On the dressing-table, standing amongst a couple of dog-eared paperbacks and some American comics, was his favourite photo of his mum. He wished she could be here with him now, and that he could talk to her like he once could.

But his mum was dead, and no amount of wishing in the world could ever bring her back. He wiped a solitary tear from his eye, and shrugged. He couldn't care less if his dad's new girlfriend was coming to visit. For all he was interested he'd stay up here in his bedroom until she'd gone.

'Your dad's my son, like you're his, Kenny,' Gran whispered softly, 'and I've got to look out for the both of you – now that your mum's gone.'

She took her grandson's hand and pulled him slowly off the bed. She smiled. 'Come downstairs and give me a hand.'

Reluctantly Kenny let himself be led downstairs. He promised he'd help his gran and be polite to – what was her name again? Sheila? But that didn't mean he was going to enjoy one second of it.

Downstairs Gran had laid the kitchen table the way she did when they were all having Sunday roast and two veg together, not when they were having Chinese takeaway from Kim's parents' new shop. A bottle of white wine had been placed in the centre of the table. There was also a jug of mineral water there too; that meant that at least his gran and grandad regarded Sheila's visit as a special occasion.

Mr Bayfield arrived from the takeaway, laden down with two carrier-bags of food. He grinned and looked at the knives and forks which Kenny had placed by each of the five plates on the table.

'You won't be needing those,' he chuckled, and took five pairs of chopsticks out of the bag. If they were going to eat Chinese food then they were going to do it the proper way, just like they did in China. Even Kenny smiled. He was a dab hand with the old chopsticks; his mum had taught him. With a bit of luck Sheila would be all fingers and thumbs and make a total idiot of herself in front of his dad. Maybe then his dad would see that no one could ever take the place of his mum.

'So how is it going, Esi?' Mr Mensah asked, as he returned to his daughter's room to take away her empty mug. He glanced over at Esi's piece of paper: apart from a couple of doodles it was still blank.

He chuckled and threw a grubby old exercise book down on her desk. Esi looked up as if to say, *What's this*?

'This is *my* story,' her father said, and opened the book. 'I got two gold stars for it!' he said proudly, and then pointed down to the comments his teacher had made at the bottom of his story. 'Well done,' she had written.

'"Well done"?' Esi wasn't impressed. She got 'well dones' for her compositions all the time.

'That was top of the roof for her,' Mr Mensah said. 'If you ever got a "good" at my school, then they made you the head teacher!'

Esi looked at the story, trying to decipher her father's tightly-spaced handwriting. 'What's it about?' she asked.

Mr Mensah sat on Esi's bed and cleared his throat. He started to read from the story he had written when he was a schoolboy.

'"Ekow came back to the house in the clearing,"' he read. '"He trod carefully and he looked hard. But the woman had gone, and her bag and all the signs that she had ever been there had gone. There wasn't even a finger-mark on a pot or a hair on the back of a chair. To tell the truth, the house had such a 'Someone gone away' feel to it that Ekow had to check three times that he had shut the door behind himself. But he had. And he was on his own, there was no one else there, and no one else was going to come. And now that he *was* on his own he felt sad and he felt empty inside, and he had the lonely feeling that he was the orphan of all the world . . ."'

Mr Mensah shut the exercise book, but Esi wanted him to read the story all over again. It had been the most beautiful story he had ever read her.

'You made it all up?' she asked breathlessly.

Her father nodded his head. 'You like it then?' Esi nodded. 'That means that there're two writers in this house, doesn't it?'

He stood up and left Esi's bedroom, leaving his old exercise book on the bed. Esi felt proud of her father. He'd written such a wonderful story. She knew that it was much better than the ones Roberta and Lyn had written for the short-story competition. If they'd had short-story competitions way back when he was a boy, she bet that her dad would have won them all, no contest.

She turned back to her own blank piece of paper, but the words wouldn't come. Perhaps it was because of hearing her father's story. It had been such a wonderful tale, that she knew that she could never write a better one.

Esi chewed the end of her pencil thoughtfully as a wild idea came into her mind. Perhaps she wouldn't have to write a better story after all . . .

The doorbell of the Bayfield house rang, and a tremor of excitement ran through the kitchen. Kenny's gran sharply whipped off her apron and started to tidy up her hair. Then she went over to Kenny and smoothed his hair as well. Even his grandad half stood to attention.

Kenny groaned. The way they were acting it was like the Queen of England had just rung the doorbell, not his dad's awful new girlfriend.

Mr Bayfield went through to the front door and opened it. From the kitchen Kenny could hear him welcoming Sheila, then he brought her through into the kitchen to be introduced.

First of all Mr Bayfield introduced her to Kenny's gran and grandad, then to Kenny himself. She smiled and reached out to shake his hand.

'I've heard a lot about you, Kenny,' she said pleasantly.

Kenny didn't reply, just looked her up and down, like he might examine something in the zoo. She was about thirty, with tidy blonde hair, and was dressed in a smart jumper and skirt.

Kenny supposed she looked all right; but she was nothing compared to his mum. His mum had been the most beautiful, kindest woman in the world; and Sheila, well – Sheila was just ordinary.

'I hear you're quite a footballer,' she continued, trying to make some conversation.

Another uncomfortable silence followed, and Kenny looked down at his shoes. In fact, he looked at anything but at the smiling face of his dad's new girl-friend.

By his side his gran tut-tutted. 'The cat got your tongue, Kenny?' she asked, and urged him to say hello.

Sheila sighed. This was awkward for her as well, and Kenny wasn't making her job any easier. She shifted her attention to the kitchen table, which Gran had decked out with a spotlessly-white tablecloth. She picked up a napkin, one of the cloth ones which Gran only used on really special occasions.

'How do you fold napkins like this, Mrs Bayfield?' she asked. 'I'm in the business and even *I* can't do one like this!'

Kenny's gran beamed with pride, and instantly warmed to the newcomer. Kenny glared at her.

'My *mum* showed her,' he said. 'She could do them better than anyone else in the world. My *mum* showed her . . .'

The meal which followed proved to be a total disaster. Throughout the next hour Kenny remained stub-bornly silent, refusing to speak to Sheila, no matter how hard she tried to make conversation. What was worse, Sheila could handle the chopsticks perfectly, almost as well as his mum used to.

His dad seemed to be all over her, filling her wine glass, passing her the bread, asking her if she was enjoying her food. They hardly even noticed him, as he poked at his sweet-and-sour prawns and rice.

His gran and grandad were just as bad too. What was wrong with them? Had they forgotten his mum so quickly?

And what if his dad and this Sheila got serious? Kenny asked himself. What if they even thought about getting married? Did that mean that his mum was going to be forgotten and that they'd never talk about her again, or remember the good times they'd shared together? And what would happen to him?

Finally he could stand it no longer. His dad and his grandparents might be betraying his mum's memory, but not him. Telling his dad that he was feeling sick, he went up to his room, leaving his meal practically untouched.

His dad and Sheila sadly watched him go. There was nothing they could do for him.

Chapter Ten

Esi stood before Mrs Clegg's desk in the empty classroom. Strictly speaking, it wasn't exactly empty. The room was full of boxes of toilet-rolls. In fact, every other classroom was packed with them as well; there were even some in the corridors. It seemed that to get things moving with the local authority you had to sign hundreds of forms at least three times, and then wait for days and days before they even bothered to reply to you . . .

On Mrs Clegg's desk there was a much smaller cardboard box. On the side of it were written the words: Short-story Competition Entries. Roberta and Lyn's entries were already in the box, and Esi added hers to the pile.

It was eight-thirty in the morning, and outside the window Esi could hear the sound of children arriving for another day at Barton Wood. She wasn't quite sure why she had come in so early today. Maybe it was because she needed time to think.

Esi knew that what she was doing was wrong, but she did so want to win the competition. Roberta and Lyn were so cocky and sure that they would win; Esi wanted to teach them a lesson.

Of course she also wanted to prove to them that when it came to writing stories she was better than both of them put together.

But it's cheating, isn't it? she scolded herself. It's not fair on the others . . . She reached out and took her story back, when a voice behind her made her jump.

'You nicking?' asked Miranda. Once again she'd managed to sneak up on someone without them hearing.

Esi relaxed. 'No!' she said.

Miranda looked at Esi disbelievingly. She pointed to the story which Esi had rolled up in her hand.

'Then what are you doing?' she asked pointedly. 'Playing teachers?'

'Mind your own!' Esi snapped. But Miranda wasn't to be put off.

'Then what are you doing?' she repeated.

'Checking my name's on my short-story entry,' Esi said, and returned the story to the box. 'For when I win!'

'You reckon you're gonna win, don't you?' Kenny asked Esi later, when they were all gathered together in the classroom. He glanced over at the box on Mrs Clegg's table. The teacher was idly flicking through some of the competition entries. Mr Skellern, who was visiting her class today, was going from group to group listening to reading.

'Yes, I reckon I am!' Esi said confidently.

Already she had forgotten about the guilty feelings she had experienced this morning. All that mattered now was winning, and showing the others just how great she was. 'Mine's brilliant!'

'Oh, modest!' Kenny said sarcastically. He couldn't be bothered with handing in an entry of his own. He had more urgent problems on his mind anyway. He carried on with his reading.

At the next table, sitting on a cardboard box of toilet rolls, Richard Skellern was having a particularly hard time encouraging Miranda to read. The story was stupid, she told him, and she wasn't going to waste her time on a load of tripe when she could be doing something much more interesting. There was the school rabbit in its little hutch to look after, for one thing.

Mr Skellern smiled, calmly took the book from her and started to read her part. That did it. Miranda snatched the book back from him and started to read. Congratulating himself on his bit of amateur psychology, he stood up and wandered over to Mrs Clegg's table, weaving in and out of the cardboard boxes.

'Shall I tiptoe through to the infants now?' he asked her, and the older teacher grinned.

'Or you could just walk normally,' she joked.

Mrs Clegg had taken quite a shine to the young enthusiastic student, and the children seemed to quite like him as well. And let's face it, she decided, anyone who could get Miranda Pudsey to read must be pretty good.

As Mr Skellern left the room, Miranda waved and shouted after him, 'Bye, Richard!'

'Miranda!' Mrs Clegg scolded. Richard Skellern might only be as old as some of their older brothers and sisters, but that was no way to talk to a teacher.

'He's only a student though, isn't he, miss?' Lee asked cheekily.

'We all have to learn our jobs, Lee,' she said, before returning to sorting out the short-story competition entries. 'Now he's going to the infants – to see how grown up they are compared to you!'

*

While his class carried on with their Victorian project, Jack Higgins was a worried man. The elegant Victorian fan that Mrs Sherry had given him for his Victorian project had gone missing. He had searched high and low for it, and had even looked in the waste-paper baskets, thinking that it might have accidentally fallen off his desk. But it was nowhere to be found.

He tried to remember when he had last seen it. Mrs Sherry had used it on the Victorian Day itself, he recalled, when she had come dressed as Queen Victoria.

After that he was sure that he had put it on the big table in the corner of the classroom, where all the other Victorian objects were displayed.

And now it had vanished, and he and Mrs Sherry were very concerned. It wasn't just that the dress shop which had lent them the fan would probably never lend them anything else again. What worried them the most was that its disappearance meant that there was a thief at work at Barton Wood.

His thoughts were interrupted when Kim tiptoed into his class, late for the second time. He shook his head as he motioned her to sit down at her normal table. Something would have to be done about Kim before it got out of hand, he decided. He resolved to have a word about her to Mrs Sherry later.

As Kim walked over to her table she passed by Mandy. Making sure that Mr Higgins wasn't watching she secretly handed over the plastic bag she was carrying.

Mandy hid it underneath her wheelchair, but not before Arjun saw the nervous and frightened look on Kim's face as she left Mandy's table.

*

Richard Skellern looked thoughtfully down at the chessboard which had been laid out on a table in the corner of the library. He was a great chess fan, and it was nice to think that there were some people at Barton Wood who were still interested in the game. A game of strategy and brainpower, he called it.

'Wotcha, sir!' chirped Lee as he entered the library. Mr Skellern noticed that he was limping.

'I'm not "sir",' he began. 'I'm Richard Skellern . . .'

'Richard!' Lee said. 'Don't they call Richards "Dicks"?'

Mr Skellern smiled. 'Perhaps "Mister Skellern" then?'

'Skellern the Melon, one of 'em called you,' Lee continued, really pushing his luck this time.

Mr Skellern chuckled in spite of himself. 'Well, at least it rhymes if nothing else . . . Shouldn't you be out to play?'

Lee pointed down to his ankle. Skellern asked him how he had hurt himself.

'Kicking Pudsey,' came the answer.

Lee looked at the chess game. 'That's a load of old baloney, isn't it? Who are you playing – the Invisible Man?'

'It's Roberta's move next.' Mr Skellern explained that he was waiting for her to join him in the game. 'She's practising for the tournament.'

The local tournament was taking place between all the schools in the area. From what Mr Skellern had heard, Roberta was going to be the only person to represent Barton Wood in the contest. After old Albert's Victorian speech everyone else was now much more interested in playing marbles!

Lee sat down at the table and studied the pieces on the board. 'I helped Roberta yesterday,' he said casually. 'Is she winning?' Mr Skellern said that she was and Lee sniggered. 'It can't be hard then!'

Mr Skellern sat down at the opposite end of the table. 'Do you want to learn a few moves?' he asked.

Lee frowned, as though he was trying to work out in which direction every one of the different pieces on the board could travel. 'You'll have to tell me the rules,' he said, and picked up one of the smaller pieces. He studied it intently. 'These are the prawns, are they?' he asked unsurely.

'*Pawns*, Lee!' Mr Skellern corrected him, and then mentally kicked himself as Lee chuckled.

'I know!' Lee said, and then winked at Mr Skellern. 'Students are *easy* wind-ups, aren't they, Dick?'

Chapter Eleven

'That's one for you, and one for you, and one for you . . .'

Mandy Willis had suddenly become one of the most popular girls in the entire school. She was sitting in her wheelchair in a corner of the playground, with several members of her class standing around her. From out of the carrier-bag that Kim had sneaked into Mr Higgins's class she was handing out lollipops. Kim was nowhere to be seen.

Mandy smiled from ear to ear. For the past few days it had seemed to her that people had been ignoring her, avoiding her even.

Now that she was giving free sweets out to everyone they were all friends with her again. It had been a great idea of hers 'persuading' Kim to bring these lollies in from her parents' takeaway.

However, as soon as everyone had received their free lollipop, and thanked her, they had all gone away, returning to their own groups. Mandy was left alone again.

Darren, Roberta James's younger brother, came up to her. 'You got any more of them sweets?' he asked.

Mandy smiled. She'd have some tomorrow, she promised.

'That's fat use!' he said, and walked off.

Mandy scowled. Everyone had been so nice to her when she first came to Barton Wood, and now it seemed as if they were pretending that she didn't even exist. Even the lollipops hadn't helped.

Arjun, the boy who had seen Kim give Mandy the bag of lollipops, finished the game of marbles he was playing and sauntered over to her. 'What's up with you?' he asked.

'What's up with *me*?' Mandy demanded, and then corrected herself. 'What's up with *everyone else*?'

'Everyone else hasn't done what you've done,' said Arjun, and before Mandy could ask him what he meant, he added, 'You never brought them lollies to school.'

'Never said I did,' she said defensively.

'You got them off Kim,' Arjun said. 'And you didn't pay her for them either . . .'

Mandy fell silent. Arjun might not say much in class, but when it came to noticing things he was really sharp.

'You've turned horrible, Mandy,' Arjun said. 'Bullying Kim for stuff and giving it out like you've bought it . . .'

What he said was true, but Mandy still refused to say anything.

'That's not going to make people like you,' he said.

'Get lost,' Mandy told him.

Arjun shook his head.

'Everyone was nice to me when I first came,' Mandy said angrily. 'Everyone was giving me hugs and making a fuss of me and giving me little pushes in my wheelchair. Now it's as if I'm like Pudsey. Everyone's around Kim now and they won't come near me.'

'It's not that,' said Arjun. He suddenly realized what the problem was. Like Mandy thought, he could be really sharp. 'You're just the same, Mandy, apart from that lolly stuff. You shouldn't have done that . . .'

Mandy smashed her fist angrily down on the side of her wheelchair. 'What is it then?' she demanded. 'Tell me!'

'Mr Higgins said not to fuss around you,' Arjun confessed. 'He said to make you more . . . on your own. That we shouldn't go around doing everything for you.'

'Is that it?' Mandy's face was a mixture of astonishment and relief. 'Do you still like me?'

'Of course we do!'

Mandy breathed a sigh of relief.

'Are you all right?' asked Roberta. She had seen Paul sitting on the edge of the sports field, by a small group of saplings which had only been planted the previous year. He was staring out into the distance and looked as if he had the weight of all the world on his shoulders.

Paul shrugged and stood up. 'I just thought I'd have a look for clues about that chest coming up,' he lied.

'You won't find any Roman footprints!' Roberta laughed.

'Don't believe in all that ghost stuff,' he said automatically.

Roberta wasn't fooled for a second. She sat down on the grass and invited Paul to join her. 'What's up?' she demanded once again. 'You've been different this week.'

Paul sighed, then told her what had happened at his

family's breakfast table a few days before. His dad had received an important-looking letter from the head office of the insurance company he worked for. In it the Managing Director had 'requested' to see him at half-past ten today.

His mum had told him and his dad not to worry – maybe they were going to promote him, or give him an increase in salary. But she was only putting off the inevitable.

His dad's firm were making redundancies right across the board. If his dad lost his job now, then they would have to sell up their house, maybe even move away from Barton Wood for good. At the very best they would have to cut down on all the little luxuries, which, for a start, meant that they couldn't afford to send Paul on the forthcoming school trip to Boddington Hall.

'He'll get something,' Roberta said hopefully. 'Your dad's like you – he's clever . . . and nice.'

She wondered if she sounded convincing or not. She knew of lots of people's parents who were out of work, and still couldn't find another job, no matter how hard they tried.

She decided that it might make things easier if she told Paul about some of her family's own troubles. What was it her parents always said? A problem shared is a problem halved?

'Darren's been acting terribly lately,' she confided in him. 'Don't tell him I said so, but he's wetting the bed, and playing up. My parents don't know what to do with him, and they're too busy . . .'

She stood up and took hold of Paul's hand and pulled him to his feet as well. She smiled. 'Come on, we can cry on each other's shoulders.'

'Paul! Roberta!' Lyn Lawrence screeched. She had caught sight of the pair of them holding each other's hands and had automatically assumed that she had just interrupted the start of a spot of something serious.

'Now I know!' she taunted.

'Shut up, Lawrence!' Roberta said angrily, and took her hand away from Paul's. Lyn continued to taunt them, and Roberta took a step forwards. 'You want trouble?' she threatened. 'You want a fist?'

Lyn's face fell, as she suddenly realized that she had gone too far. She stepped back, and then screamed.

The ground had given away beneath her feet. She tried to keep her balance and grabbed hold of one of the saplings. Lyn held on to the young tree so hard that it uprooted itself and she crashed down into a hole about a metre deep. She yelled out in pain.

Roberta and Paul rushed over to her and tried to pull her out of the hole. Richard Skellern and Mrs Clegg, who were on playground duty and had seen the accident, raced over, and together they helped to drag the screaming Lyn out of the hole. Her clothes were filthy with mud and dirt. Mr Skellern led her to a bench and sat her down on it.

'There's not many people I know who can crush the Earth's crust,' he chuckled, in an effort to raise her spirits.

But it was all in vain. Lyn continued to tremble. She hadn't fallen too far, Richard Skellern realized, but she had suffered a very nasty shock. What she really needed was the classic British remedy for shock: a nice, strong cup of tea.

Lyn glanced back at the hole; there was a look of terror in her eyes.

'It was the ghost!' she said fearfully. 'The ghost was trying to pull me down!'

Mrs Sherry, who had seen all the commotion from a classroom window, came running over the field to the small group of juniors who had already gathered around the hole.

She shooed them away and then looked thoughtfully at the hole Lyn had fallen into. The ground was obviously very weak around her. When the saplings had been planted here last year the men from the local authority clearly hadn't filled in the earth as well as they should have done.

She looked over to the time capsule which Joe had fenced off and wondered if the two things were connected. Perhaps it hadn't been vandals who had unearthed the chest after all. Perhaps it had just been a simple case of subsidence. She made a mental note to call in someone from the maintenance department to take a look at it.

'The Earth's all opening up!' wailed Lyn.

'Shh!' hissed Mr Skellern as he led Lyn away, back to the school building. 'Not so loud, or we'll have a queue of teachers waiting to jump in!'

'Mr Higgins talked to them as if I was a cabbage or something!' Mandy said to Mrs Sherry. The headteacher had discovered Mandy by herself outside the activity area when she had returned to the building, and had asked her why she was looking so upset.

'I'm sure he didn't,' Mrs Sherry said.

'Well, he talked to them behind my back, telling them how to treat me!'

Mrs Sherry sighed. She and Mr Higgins had

thought they were doing the best for Mandy. Now it seemed that they'd done more harm than good.

'We thought that they were swamping you,' she said, and knelt down by the side of Mandy's wheelchair, where she was able to look Mandy in the face.

'Your husband's disabled, isn't he?' Mandy said, and Mrs Sherry nodded. 'Does he like being pushed where you want him to go in his wheelchair? Does he like it when you have whispers about him after he's out of the way?'

'No . . .'

'I thought everyone hated me – because of you.'

Mrs Sherry shook her head. Mandy was absolutely right. It just showed that even teachers got it wrong sometimes.

'We should have talked to you first,' she admitted. 'And we should have talked to the others in front of you.' She stood up. 'I promise we'll never do it again, OK?' Mandy nodded. 'Can you forgive me?'

Mandy smiled and nodded again She knew that the teachers had just been trying to do what they thought was the best for her. The trouble with teachers was that they simply didn't know all the answers all the time.

Mrs Sherry joined Mandy in a big smile. 'Shall we kiss and make up?' she asked.

Mandy paused for a second and then said, 'No.' Mrs Sherry frowned until Mandy added, 'You wouldn't kiss me if I wasn't disabled, would you?'

Mrs Sherry chuckled. Mandy was right – as usual. Smiling to herself, she watched fondly as Mandy wheeled herself away.

*

Paul entered the kitchen of his house nervously. His mum and dad were already sitting around the kitchen table, waiting for him. A packet of chocolate biscuits was open in front of them and they were drinking cups of tea. Not glasses of champagne, as he had hoped, but plain tea from a couple of tea-bags. He looked at his dad.

'Are you out then?' he asked straight out. 'Have they done it to you?'

'Your dad's got a very generous redundancy payment,' his mother answered. 'For the first time in our lives we've got enough capital to start up something for ourselves, be our own bosses . . .'

Paul breathed a sigh of relief, and even his dad started beaming from ear to ear. His dad might be out of a job, but the money he'd got should see them right. There would be no need to leave Barton Wood and all his friends. His mum even promised that he could go to Boddington Hall with all the others. Maybe Roberta was right – his dad was clever, and he'd use the money he'd been given to create a better life for all of them.

Chapter Twelve

'Listen – I can be there by seven.' Mr Rayner cupped his hand over the telephone receiver and whispered. He looked around nervously to make sure that no one was listening.

The call had come when he, Mrs Rayner and Lee were all sitting around the breakfast table the following Monday morning. As soon as it had rung he had rushed out to take the call on the upstairs extension.

That was unusual in itself, and as Lee climbed the stairs to collect his school things he tried to eavesdrop on his dad's conversation.

'My lad, Lee, has got something on at school,' Mr Rayner continued, 'so I'll be a bit late, but you know I'm dead keen.'

Lee stopped at the top of the stairs, just out of sight of his dad, and continued to listen.

'I'm just the sort of bloke you need, Annie,' Mr Rayner said, and grinned to himself. 'Of course I haven't told them anything: I don't want them to get too worked up before we're both decided for definite. I'll see you later – and I could kiss you, I really could!'

Mr Rayner put down the phone, and rubbed his hands with glee. He was suddenly aware of Lee at the top of the stairs. Lee stared strangely at him for a second and then rushed into his bedroom to collect his schoolbag.

Lee came out of his room and ran down the stairs,

two at a time. He could hardly bring himself to look at his dad. If Mr Rayner had looked closely he might have spotted what could have been the beginnings of tears in his son's eyes.

Lee had always considered himself to be lucky. Sure, he might not always get the best marks in his tests, and he sometimes got himself into trouble, but at least his mum and dad were back together again.

And that was different to the parents of at least half the other kids at Barton Wood, who were divorced, or separated, or were in the nick, or who had never got married in the first place.

Lee was no fool. He understood in a flash who the Annie was his dad was talking to on the phone so secretly. It was a secret that Mr Rayner didn't want either Lee or his mum to know about. His dad had gone back to his old ways again: he was cheating on his mum, and on Lee himself. His dad had found himself a new girlfriend.

When Lee arrived at assembly that morning there was a buzz of excitement in the school hall. Mrs Sherry had arrived carrying an important-looking sheet of paper, and a smile on her face like a Cheshire cat's.

Everyone wondered what exciting news she had to share with the school, but it was only towards the end of assembly, after Mrs Clegg had accompanied the school on the piano in a rousing rendition of 'Any Dream Will Do', that she stepped forward to address the entire school.

'We have just received a phone call from the *Irwell Valley Recorder* about the short-story-writing competition. The judges were very impressed by the standard of the stories, particularly with a number from Barton Wood,' she said proudly. 'And one of you children will be seeing your story printed in the newspaper as the winner!'

There was a hush of anticipation in the hall. Lyn and Roberta exchanged excited glances and crossed their fingers for luck. Had one of their stories won the competition? They could hardly wait for the results. Esi also crossed her fingers – but for entirely different reasons.

'First place in the competition went to –' Mrs Sherry paused dramatically, and opened up the envelope, just like they do on TV award shows – 'Esi Mensah!'

The hall burst into applause, and several other people reached over to pat Esi on the back. Only a few wondered why she wasn't smiling.

Mrs Sherry hushed the assembly, and smiled at Esi. 'The judges said that "this unusual tale of life in a Ghanaian village revealed a vivid imagination and great storytelling ability. It was by far and away the most impressive entry".'

'Thanks to Esi,' Mrs Sherry continued, 'the school will be able to buy a splendid new computer.' Suddenly she turned serious. 'But, more importantly, Esi has brought a great deal of honour to Barton Wood. So come on, everyone – three cheers for Esi!'

The hall erupted once more, and even Mrs Clegg and Mr Higgins joined in the cheering. Esi forced a smile. Mrs Sherry and Mrs Clegg were looking at her proudly, but Esi just wished the ground would open up and swallow her.

Mrs Sherry had said that Esi had brought a great

deal of honour to Barton Wood. If only she knew the truth!

Today had started off fine for Mrs Sherry, with the news that Esi had won the short-story competition for Barton Wood. Even Mrs Swainsgate had managed to open most of the mail by break-time, and it looked as though the rest of the day was going to be problem-free. She should have known better! This was a primary school she was running, not a holiday camp!

She handed a mug of instant tea over to Richard Skellern and frowned. He had casually mentioned to her at break-time that his watch had gone missing. He'd gone into the boys' toilets to unblock a sink which Lee and Nicky had been messing around with. He'd taken his watch off and had briefly left it on the sink while he investigated a disturbance in the corridor. When he had returned, his watch had disappeared.

'I hope it hasn't been stolen,' Mrs Sherry said. 'We've never had a problem with this sort of thing at Barton Wood before . . .'

Mr Skellern shrugged. His watch hadn't been that expensive, and he couldn't see why Mrs Sherry was so worried. It would probably turn up somewhere eventually, he imagined.

As Mr Skellern left the staffroom, Mr Higgins came in and plonked himself in the seat the student teacher had just vacated. Mrs Sherry sighed. She'd come in here for a nice cuppa, but the way teachers kept coming up to her with their problems she was beginning to feel like Barton Wood's answer to Claire Rayner!

'It's Kim Lung,' Mr Higgins began. 'She fell asleep in class just now.'

'What!'

'She looks tired out most of the time,' Mr Higgins said. 'I'm beginning to think that there's something wrong there.'

Mrs Sherry frowned once again. 'I'll search out her medical form,' she promised. 'She's only been here a few days, so we should find out if she's got any specific problems before we jump to any conclusions . . .'

Mr Higgins nodded and stood up to go, but Mrs Sherry stopped him. 'Keep an eye out for a watch too, Jack,' she said. 'Mr Skellern's heirloom has gone walkies . . .'

Mr Higgins sat down gain. Unlike Richard Skellern he knew how serious this could be.

'Just like the fan,' Mrs Sherry said, reminding him of the expensive Victorian fan which had also disappeared. 'We have to be very careful how we handle this.'

'Do you have any ideas?' Mr Higgins asked.

'I've one or two thoughts . . .' Mrs Sherry said meaningfully.

Mr Higgins nodded: if there was a thief at Barton Wood, it didn't need a Sherlock Holmes to work out who the likeliest candidate was.

'Nicky Power?' he asked.

Mrs Sherry sighed. 'I hope not, Jack, I really hope not . . .'

All through break everyone had been congratulating Esi on winning the short-story competition. They'd said that she was dead clever, that she was a star. When her story was printed in next week's newspaper, she was going to be famous all over the Irwell Valley. She must be well pleased with herself.

Esi hated every second of it. As soon as morning school had ended, she had left the playground and walked home. Now she stood before the front door of her house, wondering whether she should go in or not.

What was it her dad had always said? Honesty is the best policy? Suddenly reaching a decision, Esi turned her key in the lock and entered the house.

Her dad was sitting at the kitchen table, eating his lunch and listening to Piccadilly when she walked in. He looked up curiously: it was unusual for Esi to come home for lunch.

'I need to talk to you about something . . .' Esi began. Her dad took a pile of newspapers off one of the kitchen chairs and told her to sit down.

'What's wrong?' he asked. His voice was full of concern.

Esi took a deep breath: it was now or never.

'You remember that short-story competition I entered last week?' she said. 'I've won it . . .'

Her dad whooped with joy and stood up and went over to Esi to hug her. 'That's absolutely brilliant!' he said. 'There'll be a presentation, won't there? I am so proud of you.' He switched off the radio and reached over for the telephone on the wall. 'I must ring your mother –'

'Dad, I *copied* the story you showed me!' Esi confessed.

Mr Mensah paused and replaced the receiver on its

hook. 'Well, that's OK,' he said, a little unsurely. 'It's OK writing your own version of it – that's good imagination . . .'

Esi forced herself to look her father straight in the eyes.

'You don't understand, Dad, I just wrote your story out again. I'm sorry . . .' She hung her head.

There was a long silence, and then Mr Mensah asked, 'Why?'

'I wanted to win . . .'

Mr Mensah sat down at the kitchen table again. 'Esi, nothing is worth winning if you cheat,' he said sternly. 'Your mother and I didn't bring you up to be dishonest.'

'I feel really bad,' Esi admitted. 'What can I do, Dad?'

Mr Mensah didn't say a word. It was up to Esi herself to sort out her problem the best way she could.

Chapter Thirteen

'So you cheated,' said Mrs Sherry angrily. 'What you've done is the worst kind of deceit!'

Esi suddenly felt about two inches tall. She was really ashamed of herself.

'Do you realize for one second the trouble you've caused?'

'I'm sorry, miss . . .' Esi muttered. Her dad had been right: it wasn't always easy telling the truth.

'Sorry isn't good enough,' Mrs Sherry snapped, and then her voice softened. 'What about the presentation? The *Irwell Valley Recorder* is sending around a reporter *and* a photographer. What do I say to them? That the child who won is a cheat and a liar? You've let me down, Esi. You've let the school down. But more than that, you've let *yourself* down!'

Esi knew that Mrs Sherry was right. Why couldn't she have written her own story? Then if she had won the competition she would have had something to be really proud of. Instead, she just felt miserable and humiliated.

'I'll speak to the editor and try to smooth things over,' Mrs Sherry said, and then added, 'You've forced me into a situation where I'm going to have to tell a lie to the whole school – and I don't like that one little bit!'

Mrs Sherry's lie came later that day in Mrs Clegg's classroom. There was a stern and frosty look on her face as she addressed the whole class. To Esi, however, it seemed that she was speaking to her alone.

'I'm afraid I have a piece of rather bad news,' she began. 'There's been a mix-up about the short-story competition . . . I'm afraid I got my wires crossed and Esi Mensah's story didn't win.' She looked pointedly at Esi, before saying, 'Although she did get into the final six . . .'

Roberta, who was sitting at her table, gave Esi a sympathetic pat on the back. 'That's really rotten luck,' she said. Esi just shrugged.

'The competition was won by a story from Mill Bank school,' Mrs Sherry announced. A couple of boys booed. 'But maybe next time we'll have a winner.'

She walked out of the classroom, but not before giving Esi a sharp and meaningful look. Esi bowed her head, relieved that her ordeal was finally over. Being honest hurt, but at least it meant that she'd no longer be troubled by those horrible feelings of guilt.

Lyn came over. 'I bet your story really was the best,' she said in an effort to cheer Esi up.

Esi shook her head firmly. 'No,' she said. 'I didn't deserve to win.'

Lee licked his lips thoughtfully as he tried to concentrate on the chessboard in front of him. He knew he was losing his game with the boy from St Paul's. What made it even worse was that, on the other side of the hall, Roberta was racing towards a victory with her opponent. Roberta was by far the best player in the chess tournament, but even so, he didn't want to appear a dilk in front of her, and anyway, he hadn't been playing chess for as long as her.

He moved his king on to a white space, and then

instantly regretted what he'd done. The St Paul's boy sniggered, and shifted his bishop into a strategic position two squares away from his king.

'Checkmate!' the St Paul's boy said in that smug and posh voice with which everyone at his school seemed to speak.

Lee smiled, all sportsman-like, and shook his opponent's hand. He got up and walked over to his mum, who had come to watch the game as she had promised. Lee's dad was nowhere to be seen, and Lee had a pretty good idea where he might be. That phone call he had overheard this morning had been playing on his mind all day.

Mrs Rayner smiled sympathetically. 'Hard luck,' she said. 'Don't worry – your dad'll be here for your next match. I'll pop outside and see if I can see him.'

And with that Mrs Rayner left the hall, leaving Lee alone. From the other side of the hall, Richard Skellern spotted him and sauntered over, leaving Mrs Sherry and Mr Higgins to watch Roberta thrash her opponent.

Mr Skellern could see that something was bothering Lee, and it wasn't just being defeated by the boy from St Paul's. He might only be a student, but Mr Skellern liked to think that there were times when he understood the pupils at Barton Wood better than the real teachers like Mrs Clegg or Mr Higgins. After all, at twenty-one he was only a couple of years older than the big brothers of some of his pupils.

'Are you absolutely sure?' he asked Lee, after Lee had started to tell him about his dad's secret phone call that morning. 'Are you absolutely sure that your dad's . . . well, you know . . .'

'Mucking about,' Lee said helpfully, sparing the student's blushes. 'I heard him on the phone to *her* . . . What should I do? Should I tell my mum?'

'Er, well, I'm . . . I'm not really sure,' Mr Skellern stammered.

He'd never been in a situation like this before: he was slowly becoming aware that being a teacher meant more than just marking tests and keeping order in the classroom.

'You don't know much, do you, sir?' Lee sneered. He'd already reached his own decision without help from any teachers or grown-ups. Mrs Rayner came back, and Mr Skellern made a quick exit.

'There's no sign of him yet,' she said, and added hopefully, 'I'm sure he's got a good reason for not being here . . .'

Lee wasn't convinced. 'Can we go home now, Mum?'

'But you've got another game to play!' Mrs Rayner protested.

'I don't feel in the mood,' Lee said. 'Can we just go home now? There's . . . there's something I've got to tell you . . .'

Mrs Rayner looked at the clock on the kitchen wall. It was a quarter past nine. She continued washing her dishes, scrubbing them with such a force that it was a marvel that none of them had broken. At the kitchen table Lee was idly toying with a half-eaten sandwich.

The front door slammed shut, and Lee and his mum exchanged anxious looks. The moment Mr Rayner walked into the kitchen he could see that something was wrong. He held up his hands in apology.

'OK, I'm sorry I didn't make the chess tournament,' he said. 'I had a bit of business to attend to and it took longer than I thought.'

'And the rest . . .'

Mrs Rayner was standing with her arms folded, her face red with rage. She looked over to Lee by the table. 'Lee – bed!'

'Wait a minute!' Mr Rayner said to Lee, who was already shuffling out of the room. 'You haven't told me how you got on!'

'He lost,' said Mrs Rayner frostily. 'He wasn't concentrating – he was too busy worrying about you!'

Mr Rayner fell silent and Lee walked out of the kitchen, pulling the door behind him. He made sure to leave it a little ajar though.

Mr Rayner looked at his wife. He still wasn't quite sure why she was looking so angry and why Lee had been so miserable and silent.

'Look, I really am sorry about missing the chess,' he said to his wife, 'but it was something important . . .'

'*Somebody* important,' Mrs Rayner said. 'Lee told me. You let your son down to go off with some fancy woman! And I thought you'd changed!'

'What?'

'Don't start trying to deny it! You're up to your old tricks again! Who is she?'

Mr Rayner tried to put his arm around her but she pushed him away. 'You've got the wrong end of the stick, love,' he said.

'Lee heard you!' she shouted. 'He heard you making your sordid little arrangements with her!'

For a second Mr Rayner was dumbfounded, still not understanding what his wife was talking about. And then it dawned on him, and a huge smile appeared on his face.

'I was sorting out a job!' he said.

'Of course you were,' Mrs Rayner said sarcastically. There was a note of uncertainty in her voice though, as if she really wanted to believe him.

'Annie – the woman I went to see tonight – runs a haulage company,' Mr Rayner said. 'She's sixty years old and built like a wrestler. She and her brother have a fleet of lorries doing local work and I went to see them to talk about a job.'

Mrs Rayner still wasn't totally convinced. 'So why didn't you mention any of this before?' she asked.

'I didn't want to get your hopes up. I wanted to check it out first before I told you,' he said, and then chuckled. 'And now I've cracked it! So are you going to congratulate me or not?'

Mrs Rayner suddenly felt very foolish. And very relieved. And very happy. With tears of joy streaming down her face she went over and gave her husband an enormous hug.

'I thought I was going to lose you again,' she sobbed.

'My messing-about days are through,' he promised her. 'You and Lee are not going to lose me – and certainly not to a sixty-year-old with tattoos on her forearms!'

He was suddenly aware of Lee, who had been listening behind the door. He grinned.

'Did you get all that then, Lee?' he called out.

Behind the door Lee nodded, and brushed at his eyes. Yes, he had sure got that all right!

Chapter Fourteen

'You haven't forgotten the kitchen sink, have you?' Olive Swainsgate asked jokingly.

'I've already packed it,' replied Mrs Sherry. Instead of her usual smart suit she was dressed in a sloppy jumper and a pair of jeans. She looked around at the chaos in her office.

Cardboard boxes were piled high on the floor and her desk was cluttered with all manner of things. There were first-aid kits, clipboards, writing materials and exercise books. There was even a plastic sick-bucket. Hidden somewhere amongst them was her own battered suitcase. It was the first day of the school trip to Boddington Hall, and even though she hadn't set off yet Mrs Sherry wished that it was all over. It was like organizing a military operation just getting twenty-odd schoolchildren, plus herself and Len Bamber, off to Boddington Hall, the education authority's residential activity centre, way out in the country.

Handing a clipboard to Mrs Swainsgate, and telling her to check off all the items she had brought, Mrs Sherry went out to the car-park to supervise the boarding of the hired coach. Councillor Bamber had already arrived. Wearing a parka and a daft-looking bobble-cap, he was busy trying to organize everyone himself. Needless to say he wasn't meeting with a great deal of success.

By the school entrance a crowd of parents had

gathered to see their children off and help them with their luggage. Michael Bayfield was there, making sure that Kenny had packed everything he needed into his rucksack, even though Gran must have checked it already seven thousand times that morning.

Nearby, Mrs Mensah, dressed in her nurse's uniform ready for work, was helping Esi put her bag in the luggage space underneath the waiting coach. Nicky, meanwhile, was being seen off by Tracey, who couldn't believe her luck in being free of her younger brother for three whole days. The only person from the top class noticeable by her absence was Miranda; but then, as Mrs Sherry realized, Mrs Pudsey could hardly afford to send her daughter on the school trip. She'd have probably considered it a waste of time and money. So for the next few days Miranda would stay and help out in Mr Higgins's class.

Everyone turned as a mini drove up to the school entrance. Kenny glared daggers as Sheila jumped out of the car. She ran up to his father and gave him a peck on the cheek. Lee and Nicky and all the others looked appreciatively at the good-looking blonde, but Kenny scowled. Could Sheila not even leave him and his dad alone here? What was she trying to do? Make out she was his mum or something?

Satisfied that everything was proceeding as well as could be expected, even with the 'help' of Len Bamber, Mrs Sherry returned to her office. Mr Higgins was waiting for her.

She raised a surprised eyebrow as she saw that her deputy was wearing a smart blue suit. Mr Higgins was to be acting head for the three days that she was away: it seemed that he was already dressing for the part! He was carrying a large notebook, which he had bought this morning from the newsagents on Pennington Road. His pen was poised, ready to take down any instructions from Mrs Sherry.

'Anything last minute, Chris?' he asked her.

Mrs Sherry consulted her clipboard. 'Chase up grounds maintenance,' she said. 'They still haven't sent anybody about the holes in the field.' The last thing she wanted when she got back from Boddington Hall was to find that the entire school had subsided and sunk beneath the ground.

'The kids are convinced that it's a Roman centurion digging through the soils of time,' Mr Higgins reminded her, but jotted it down in his notebook anyway.

'That's probably more sensible than anything grounds maintenance could dream up,' she remarked wryly, and remembered all the trouble she had had in finally getting rid of the boxes of toilet-rolls that had been delivered to the school. It had taken a couple of letters and some angry phone calls before they had even bothered to send their men round with a van.

She finally located her suitcase amongst all the cardboard boxes in the office. Three days away from Barton Wood! Free of worried parents, even more worried teachers, and tales of things that go bump in the night on the playing field. And if there was one thing she wanted to leave behind at Barton Wood it was all this rubbish about Roman ghosts.

Mrs Sherry should have known better. Even as she carried her suitcase out to the car-park Nicky and Lee were deep in conversation on the back seat of the coach. And they had only one thought on their minds: ghosts!

Mr Higgins waved goodbye to the coach for Boddington Hall as it finally eased its way out of the car-park and on to the main road. He walked back into the school building, looking forward to the next three days. He was going to be in charge of Barton Wood school, and he was determined that everything would run like clockwork. When Mrs Sherry returned, he promised himself, there would be no more talk of ghosts, no holes in the school field, and, with a little bit of luck, he might even discover who had uprooted the time capsule as well.

However, all those problems could wait: first of all, he had to deal with Kim. He had been concerned about her lateness and her lack of attention in class for a week now. Mrs Sherry had checked the young Vietnamese girl's medical records, but there was no evidence in them to suggest that there was anything wrong with her.

However, Mrs Sherry had given him a lift home last night after the chess tournament, and they had driven past Kim's parents' takeaway. It had been about half-past nine, and from the car window they had seen Kim working behind the counter. So Jack Higgins's first task as acting head of Barton Wood was to call Mr Lung, Kim's father, into his office.

'She was fast asleep in class,' Mr Higgins told Mr Lung. The Vietnamese man was sitting in the big easy chair in Mrs Sherry's office, which she always reserved for visitors.

'She does stay up sometimes,' Mr Lung admitted. 'She loves reading her schoolbooks . . .'

'Actually I was wondering about her working in the shop, Mr Lung,' Mr Higgins said as tactfully as he could. 'I was passing by quite late last night and I did see her serving . . . Is it possible for someone else to do Kim's work in the evenings?'

Mr Lung shook his head and sighed. 'Mr Higgins, I know how it must look to you,' he said, a little guiltily. 'But we don't approve of Kim working in the shop, and we do try and make her go to bed at a decent hour. But sometimes she can't sleep . . .'

Mr Higgins was instantly concerned.

'We are Vietnamese, Mr Higgins,' Kim's father continued. 'We are also what you call "Boat People".'

Mr Higgins became slightly embarrassed. He'd read about the Boat People in the newspapers years ago. They were the refugees who'd left Vietnam in tiny boats in the 1970s to find a new and sometimes better life in the West.

'What does that mean?' asked Mr Lung, although it was clear that he wasn't expecting an answer from Mr Higgins. 'It means a beach in Vietnam, and soldiers looking for us on the blackest night there ever was . . . They threw us into the boats, pushed us, split us up. It was too dark to see and there was all this calling, mothers calling out for their children.

'Twenty-three went from our village, Mr Higgins. Only nine arrived in England . . .'

Mr Higgins shuddered as Mr Lung continued. Kim, he told him, had been born in a resettlement camp and was as British as any of the teachers at Barton Wood.

'But Kim asked us about how we got here. And we told her about that night when the soldiers came ... Perhaps we told her too much and now she dreams ... Maybe she dreams that she is left on that beach in that darkness. And that's when she comes down to the shop, down to the noise, the lights and us ...'

Mr Higgins placed a reassuring hand on Mr Lung's as if to say that he understood.

'I'm sorry, Mr Higgins,' the Vietnamese man said, 'but we are so grateful that Kim is there to come down to us, that we let her ...'

Mrs Sherry dropped Len Bamber's heavy suitcase down on to the gravel path and looked up at the signpost in front of the big old country house. It read:

Boddington Hall
Field Studies Unit
Irwell Valley Education Authority
Warden: F. R. Langley, B.Sc.

She breathed in deeply of the fresh country air: the smell of trees and freshly-mown grass made a big change from the petrol fumes of Barton Wood. She hoped that Nicky and Lee and all the others appreciated it. For several of them, these three days at Boddington Hall would be the first time they had lived in the country. For many, it would also be their first time away from home and their parents.

And Mrs Sherry knew what that meant. So too did Nicky and Lee, if the looks on their faces were any indication. Mrs Sherry resolved to keep a close eye on them, somehow knowing that if there was going to be any trouble or pranks at Boddington Hall, then Nicky and Lee were sure to be behind it all.

She silently congratulated herself on surviving the forty-mile coach journey into the countryside with as few disasters as possible. In fact, if she forgot about Councillor Bamber throwing up in the sick-bucket about half a dozen times on the way here, it had been a relatively uneventful journey.

In fact, it was very easy to forget about Len Bamber, especially as they had lost him. He'd left the coach on their journey stop (to throw up again), and when it had been time to go off again he was nowhere to be found. Nicky, of course, had announced to everyone that the Roman ghost of Barton Wood had captured him. There had been no time to wait for him, so their coach had driven off without him.

Councillor Bamber could make his own way to Boddington Hall later, Mrs Sherry had told Barton Wood. He was a grown man after all, even though at times he acted more like a child.

She turned back to the children, who were sorting out their pieces of luggage. The coach was already pulling out of the drive, heading up the hill back to town. She clapped her hands, trying to attract everyone's attention.

'OK, children,' she began, and then stopped as the piercing sound of a whistle filled the air. Everyone, including Mrs Sherry, stopped what they were doing and looked in the direction from which the sound had come.

A military-looking middle-aged man was coming

down the steps of the big house to meet them. He was dressed in a sensible corduroy jacket and trousers and in his hand he carried a clipboard. Around his neck there was a whistle on a string.

He stopped and looked at Mrs Sherry and her collection of pupils from Barton Wood. Clearly he was very unimpressed by them.

'Right! The tallest on the left!' he barked. 'The smallest on the right! Now, *move!*'

Two or three people sniggered at the newcomer. Several others looked over to Mrs Sherry, for some idea of what to do. But Mrs Sherry was just as taken aback by the man's military manner as they were.

Disappointed, the middle-aged man shook his head. He strode up to Esi. 'Do they sell cotton buds in Barton Wood?' he asked her. 'You know – those little sticks with cotton on them?'

Esi smiled. 'I think they do –' she began.

'Then why haven't you lot used them to clean your earholes out!' he bellowed, making everyone, including Mrs Sherry, jump. 'I said the tallest to the left and the smallest to the right!'

Everyone sprang into action and formed a line, just like the man had ordered them to. Mrs Sherry almost joined the line, but instead walked up to the man and introduced herself.

'And I'm Fred Langley, the warden here,' he said in a much quieter voice, and smiled. 'It's nice to meet you.' He looked around and frowned. 'I thought you had a male teacher with you?'

Mrs Sherry smiled. 'Len Bamber, our Chairman of Governors,' she said. 'He got lost . . .'

Fred Langley shook his head. He was about to say

that he wasn't surprised that the Barton Wood children were such a disorganized lot, if their own governors couldn't find their way to Boddington Hall. Then he noticed Kenny. He was standing at the far right end of the line, next to Nicky and Lee, even though he was a good twelve centimetres shorter than either of them.

'Where do you think you're going, Goliath?' Mr Langley asked loudly. Several people laughed as Mr Langley moved Kenny to the short end of the line, next to Esi and Roberta.

'There goes a year of confidence-building,' Mrs Sherry said to Mr Langley when he returned to her.

Mr Langley gave her his most dazzling smile. 'Trust me,' he said. 'By the end of the week they'll be wanting to take me home! But if I go too far, just let me know . . .'

Mrs Sherry looked over at Kenny. He was glaring at the warden, furious at having been made an example of in front of all his mates.

'Just cut the Goliath jokes and it's a deal,' she said.

Fred Langley nodded, and strode up to the class again. He looked just like a crusty sergeant-major inspecting his troops.

'My name is Mr Langley,' he announced, 'but you can all call me . . . Mr Langley.' Esi, Roberta and several others started to laugh until Mr Langley shouted, 'And I will tell you when to laugh!'

'That line-up just now was appalling!' he told them. 'You're the worst school I've had here since 1823!'

Everyone looked nervously at each other, unsure whether the warden had just told a joke or not. No one dared to laugh, or even smile.

'Now, Boddington Hall is going to be your home for the next three days,' he continued. 'It's my home always. It is clean and tidy and *nothing* is broken. And when you lot go home it will be clean and tidy and *nothing* will be broken!'

Mrs Sherry sighed to herself. If Fred Langley really believed that then he was going to be in for a rude awakening! Of that she was sure.

Nicky and Lee crept down the dark, empty first-floor corridors of Boddington Hall, dressed all in black like two cat burglars. Their eyes darted nervously this way and that, to make sure that no one was watching them.

Nicky glanced at his watch: it was eight o'clock. Downstairs they could hear Mrs Sherry addressing a small group in the lounge; but of Langley there was no sign. If he caught them they would be in serious trouble.

They finally reached the door with the sign which read *Girls 1*. Quick as a flash they sneaked into the room.

The room was in darkness, but, from the light of the full moon, they could make out the row of four bunk-beds. Lee walked up to the first one.

'Which one's Roberta's?' he whispered, and then recognized her jacket, which she had thrown on to the top of her bed. While Nicky kept watch by the open door, he took something out of the bag he was carrying over his shoulder.

'Hurry up!' Nicky hissed, and joined Lee by the bunk-bed. 'Langley might come in!'

Suddenly the lights were switched on. Both boys

froze, and then slowly turned around. Esi and Roberta were standing in the open doorway.

'Come to see us, have you?' Roberta asked sarcastically, and moved over to her bed.

'Sherry's waiting for us downstairs,' Nicky said nervously. He moved towards the doorway, but Roberta called him back.

She pulled back her bedclothes and took out the object that Lee had hidden there. She tut-tutted like her mum always did when she caught Darren doing something particularly childish.

'I think this is yours,' she said, and handed Lee back the head of the Roman centurion.

Lee and Nicky looked despairingly at each other. Their plan to frighten the girls had failed. Nicky picked up the dummy's head and put it in his bag before following the others downstairs.

'Tomorrow we're going to see what you're *really* made of,' Mr Langley announced to Barton Wood. 'We're all going for a hike over the tarn.'

Everyone looked at their own copy of the map that Mr Langley had given them. It showed the large lake, or tarn, on the hills outside Boddington Hall.

'Get plenty of sleep tonight, because you're all going to need it tomorrow!' Mr Langley told them. 'Breakfast is at 0630 hours!'

Everyone groaned. Even Mrs Sherry wasn't looking forward to getting up so early, especially as she had to wait for Mr Bamber to show up at the Hall.

She'd finally received a phone call from the Councillor, who had sheepishly told her that he'd got on the wrong coach at the journey stop and fallen asleep.

When he'd woken up he'd discovered that he was on a pensioners' outing to Rhyll in North Wales. He said he'd hitchhike on to Boddington Hall, so it was anyone's guess what time he would arrive.

When Mr Langley had left, Lee called out to Mrs Sherry, 'Did you know that Boddington Hall was haunted, miss?'

By his side Lyn shivered, and Mrs Sherry sighed. 'Stop that nonsense, Lee,' she snapped.

Lee shrugged. 'I just thought that the girls should know,' he said. He turned to Lyn, who was already feeling a little scared in this big old spooky house. 'Be ready when the temperature drops, when the groaning starts and when the horrible face appears at the window.'

There was a tap at the window, and Lee screamed. There was a face at the window, out there in the darkness. It was a face so horrible that Lee could not have imagined it even in his wildest nightmares.

He looked this way and that, unsure which way to turn. Then the face at the window tapped again, and Lee wondered why everyone, including Lyn, was laughing at him.

He looked at the face at the window again.

'Will somebody let me in?' came a plaintive voice.

Mr Bamber had finally arrived at Boddington Hall.

Chapter Fifteen

Bleary-eyed, Mrs Sherry looked at her watch. It was six-thirty in the morning and she was sitting in the dining-room of Boddington Hall. A barely touched bowl of Bran Flakes was in front of her. Fred Langley had woken everyone up for breakfast thirty minutes ago, but all Mrs Sherry wanted to do was crawl back into her bed.

She looked around at the others in the dining-room. It was obvious that they all felt the same. The only person who seemed to have any life in her was Lyn, who was eagerly going around the room, scooping the leftovers from people's plates and greedily wolfing them down.

Councillor Bamber was missing. But then it was said that nothing short of a direct nuclear hit could wake up Len Bamber when he was asleep.

Mr Langley was standing by the serving hatch, watching them all like a general inspecting his troops. He looked as fresh as a daisy. But then, Mrs Sherry reflected, he hadn't been kept up half the night by 'ghosts' appearing outside the window of the girls' dormitory, or children feeling homesick, or a boys v. girls pillow-fight on the landing at half-past three in the morning.

Mrs Sherry would have been quite happy to curl up and die at this moment; as it was, she was having as much difficulty in keeping awake as Roberta, whose sleepy head was already sinking on to Nicky's shoulder.

'Roberta James, sit up!' Mrs Sherry said loudly, and then wished that she hadn't. Raising her voice was doing her headache no good at all.

'If you want to go to sleep, do it at night! Do not keep me up till three-thirty a.m. and then expect to sleep over breakfast!' She stood up angrily, and pushed her bowl of Bran Flakes away. 'And that goes for everyone!' she cried.

Everyone looked warily at Mrs Sherry; even Roberta sat up. It was rare for Mrs Sherry to lose her temper with them. They all thought it must be her new surroundings. After all, the country air did strange things to some people.

'Some of you are spoiling it for us all,' Mrs Sherry continued. She named no names, but looked pointedly at Lee and Nicky: she knew exactly who had scared Mr Bamber half to death last night, by hiding the 'ghost's' head in his bathroom. 'We're here to try new things, to have new experiences and to enjoy the fresh air and the scenery. And you can't do that on just two hours' sleep.'

There was a murmur of agreement on that. Nicky even thought of putting his hand up and asking if that meant that they could all go back to bed, but thought better of it.

'You're going to be walking seven miles today,' she informed them, in a tone of voice which suggested that even she wasn't looking forward to it. 'And some of you won't last seven minutes.'

Right on cue, Paul let out an enormous yawn. Fred Langley marched up to his table.

'How dare you yawn in my dining-room?' he bellowed. He turned back to Mrs Sherry. 'Please continue.'

'If behaviour doesn't improve, Barton Wood, then we're going home,' Mrs Sherry warned.

A couple of children looked as though that might not be such a bad idea after all. Even Lee and Nicky wondered if it might not be better swapping their late-night terrorizing of the girls for a lie-in till half-past seven and then bacon and eggs in front of the telly watching *The Big Breakfast*.

The door to the dining-room swung open and an attractive and fresh-faced girl walked in. Immediately all the boys sat up. They decided that they liked it at Boddington Hall after all.

The girl was in her early twenties and was wearing a baggy sweater and a pair of tight, figure-hugging jeans. A couple of boys gave her a wolf-whistle. Roberta looked angrily at Lee, who was obviously very taken by the new arrival.

Mr Langley introduced the girl as Laurie Harrison, his assistant leader on the day's hike. He went off to the kitchens, leaving Mrs Sherry with Laurie, who went over to the nearest table and poured herself a cup of tea from the pot. Several pairs of boys' eyes followed her every move.

'So we're off to the tarn today,' she said casually, and then glanced towards the departing figure of Mr Langley. 'Has Fred been on form today?'

Mrs Sherry nodded.

'They'll love him in the end,' Laurie promised her.

'So he keeps telling me.' Mrs Sherry smiled. 'But he's running out of time!'

'His bark's bad,' said Laurie, and started to butter a slice of toast. 'But he never bites!'

'You could have fooled me,' Mrs Sherry chuckled.

Just then the canteen door opened and Len Bamber walked in. Unshaven, unwashed, and unhappy at having to get up so early, he looked as though he had been dragged backwards through one of the hedges which surrounded Boddington Hall.

When he saw Laurie talking to Mrs Sherry, he grinned: suddenly Boddington Hall looked like it might be fun after all. He turned and raced out of the dining-room.

He returned fifteen minutes later. Now he was impeccably dressed, wearing a smart cravat, a freshly-ironed shirt and a smart blazer. He had combed and slicked back his hair. He sneaked a look at his reflection in one of the windows and decided he looked pretty good. No, better than pretty good, he corrected himself: irresistible!

Mr Bamber swaggered over to Laurie and Mrs Sherry. As he passed Lee's table, Lee smelt the Councillor's aftershave, and asked loudly, 'Cor, who's blocked the drains up then?'

Len Bamber ignored him and reached out his hand to Laurie. Trying hard to stop herself from laughing, Mrs Sherry introduced the two.

'How lovely to meet you,' Mr Bamber said huskily.

Mrs Sherry couldn't help but smile.

'What time do we have to be out?' Lee asked Kenny, who was sitting on the edge of his bed, packing a couple of cans of Coke into his rucksack.

Kenny looked at his watch. It was nine o'clock now; they were due to start on their hike in thirty minutes.

'Langley's coming round to inspect the dorms in

ten minutes,' Paul reminded them. He was busy tidying up his things and making up the covers on his bed.

He looked over at Nicky, who was standing on his own bed, trying to judge the distance between it and Paul's. He reckoned that he could just make it.

'Come on, Power,' Paul said impatiently. 'Langley's going to kill us if he finds the place like this!'

'OK,' Nicky said cheerfully. 'Here I come!'

Letting out a whoop worthy of Tarzan of the Apes, Nicky leapt through the air and landed on Paul's bed. There was an enormous *crack!* as the bed broke under Nicky's weight.

All four boys exchanged terrified looks. That was it: they were really going to be in for it now!

Nicky, Lee, Kenny and Paul rushed outside into the cold morning air, where Laurie was already lining up the rest of Barton Wood ready for the hike. Laurie smiled at what she thought was their eagerness to join in. She handed each of them special waterproof trousers and tops. You could never trust the weather on a long walk, she told them.

Esi and Roberta looked suspiciously at the boys. From the worried looks on their faces they knew that something was up. As Laurie went off to greet Mrs Sherry and Mr Bamber, who were carrying plastic containers with today's lunch, the four boys huddled together.

'Go on – tell her,' Paul said, and pointed to Laurie. 'She'll be better than Langley . . .'

Nicky shook his head. 'She'll tell him, won't she,

you dilk?' he said. 'Let's leave it – he might not spot it . . .'

'Not spot it! You've broken the stupid bed in two!'

Nicky fell silent as he tried to think of some way out of their situation. Suddenly he heard the main door of the hall slam, and saw Fred Langley thundering down the steps to their line. His face was bright-red with anger.

Kenny gave Nicky a look which seemed to say, *You're in for it now, mate!*

Laurie, Mrs Sherry and Len Bamber all looked puzzled, wondering what was going on.

Mr Langley marched up to the line. 'Would any boy like to tell me anything?' he asked. No reply. Nicky frowned, trying to pretend that he didn't know what the warden was talking about.

Mr Langley repeated his question, and, when there was no answer again, he threw back his head and roared with rage. 'There is a bunk *completely* destroyed in your *tip* of a dormitory – and it will cost at least a hundred pounds to replace!'

A horrible silence fell. Everybody remembered what Mrs Sherry had told them at breakfast that morning. If there was any more trouble then they would all be sent back home to Barton Wood in disgrace!

Mr Langley tapped his foot impatiently and looked at Nicky and the others.

'Who was it!' he demanded. 'Who broke the bed?'

Nicky shuffled awkwardly but didn't say anything. Lee, Kenny and Paul looked down at their shoes: they weren't going to grass on their mate.

'Well, who was it?' Langley asked again.

There was an embarrassed cough, and Councillor Bamber came forward. There was a sheepish grin on his face.

'It was me, actually,' he said. 'I was testing it for one of the lads and it just snapped.' He patted his stomach. 'Too much Yorkshire pud, I'm afraid . . .'

He took a chequebook and pen from the inside pocket of his blazer. 'I was going to mention it later. It was a hundred pounds, wasn't it? I am sorry – but accidents do happen.'

He quickly glanced over at Nicky and his friends, who couldn't believe what was happening. 'Don't they, boys?' Mr Bamber said meaningfully before turning back to Mr Langley.

The warden told Councillor Bamber to put away his chequebook. 'I'll repair it myself,' he said, and added grumpily, 'It'll take precious time, but I'll do it . . .'

Councillor Bamber beamed, and promised to give the warden a hand later that night. As he returned to Mrs Sherry and Laurie he winked slyly at the boys.

They were standing there, open-mouthed and wide-eyed. What did you know? they seemed to be saying. Looks like Bamber is a human being after all!

'Let's get those kits on!' Mr Langley said, trying to re-establish his authority. Everyone started to slip into the unfamiliar waterproof clothing which went over their normal clothes. Kenny, in particular, had the most difficulty.

'What are you doing, boy?' Mr Langley asked gruffly. 'Who gets you dressed – your mother?'

Another deadly silence descended on everyone, and Mr Langley knew that he'd said something wrong.

Kenny stared up hatefully at him, and the girls began to mutter amongst themselves.

Mr Langley turned as he felt Mrs Sherry's hand on his shoulder. She wasn't smiling either; in fact she looked furious. She led him away from Kenny and the others, and into the building.

'You asked me to tell you if you went too far,' Mrs Sherry said angrily as soon as they were inside. 'Well, you just did!'

'I have to be hard on them,' he said calmly. 'On any activity, from rock-climbing to walking, I must be able to get an instant response – it could save a life.' He shrugged. 'I try to have a little joke too . . .'

'*Joke?*' Mrs Sherry shouted. 'That was a joke?' She forced herself to calm down. 'Fred, I understand why you're so strict, and safety is at the top of *my* list too. But Kenny wasn't climbing a rock-face. He was just involved in his usual battle – trying to get over the death of his mother . . .'

Mr Langley was taken aback. 'I had no idea . . .'

'He hasn't got a mother to get him dressed, for goodness' sake!' Mrs Sherry exploded, losing her temper again.

'I really am sorry . . .'

'Of course,' Mrs Sherry said, through clenched teeth. 'But it's surely worth thinking *before* you rip into someone like that, isn't it? You never know their circumstances.'

'I am sorry,' Mr Langley said, and meant it. 'And I will apologize to the boy.'

Mrs Sherry nodded approvingly. She knew that Fred Langley wasn't a bad sort and that his heart was in the right place. It was just that he went about things in a different way. The trouble was, that way wasn't always the right way for everyone.

'I don't know how you instil discipline at Barton Wood . . .' he began, but Mrs Sherry stopped him.

'At Barton Wood, discipline comes from warm relationships and mutual respect,' she said. 'And, Fred, this morning you've just lost both . . .'

Back at Barton Wood Mr Higgins was settling into his new job as acting headteacher. He enjoyed the responsibility and the sense of importance he felt when the other teachers came to the office to ask his opinion on things. He'd even been given the task of organizing the forthcoming school fête while Mrs Sherry was away, and he was determined to do an excellent job.

His head filled with daydreams, he marched down the corridor carrying a roll of posters advertising the school fête. He stopped at the notice-board to pin up one of the posters and, from out of the corner of his eye, he spotted Darren. Roberta's younger brother was rummaging among the coats in the nearby cloak-room area. Mr Higgins stood still, so that Darren wouldn't notice him, and watched.

Darren looked nervously around, to make sure that no one was spying on him. Then he quickly whipped out a pair of plastic swimming-goggles from one of the coats on the hooks.

Mr Higgins watched as Darren tiptoed down the corridor to the rabbit hutch on one of the activity tables. He opened the hutch and shoved the goggles inside, disturbing the school's pet rabbit, who thought that Miranda had come to take him out and stroke him. Darren quickly shut the hutch door and raced off down the corridor back to his class.

When he had gone Mr Higgins walked over to the hutch. He was puzzled. He knew that Mrs Clegg was taking her class to the swimming-baths later that day, which explained the presence of the goggles. But the coat Darren took them from definitely wasn't his own. Wondering if Darren was playing a practical joke on one of his mates, Mr Higgins opened up the rabbit hutch again.

As he took out the swimming-goggles, the rabbit gently nuzzled his hand. Mr Higgins scratched the animal behind its ear, and then his hand touched something cold and metallic buried in the rabbit's straw bedding.

Frowning, Mr Higgins took the object out. He already knew what it was.

Hidden in the rabbit's hutch was Richard Skellern's missing watch and the Victorian fan. That could mean only one thing . . .

Darren James was the thief of Barton Wood.

Richard Skellern looked uncertainly at the water of the swimming-pool and stayed well away from the edge. The water here looked very deep and he couldn't swim. He'd always meant to learn, but had somehow never got round to it.

He glanced over at the younger children who were swimming about in the water like pairs of fishes, under the watchful eye of Mrs Clegg and a lifeguard.

Even Mandy was having a great time in the water: it was the one place where she didn't need her wheel-chair and where she could move about just as freely as all the other children. It was such a shame that Barton Wood didn't have the money to build its own swimming-pool; then she could have gone swimming every day.

'Someone's nicked my goggles, sir,' Liam said.

Mr Skellern, who was more concerned with keeping as far away from the water as possible, didn't hear him. He looked down at Liam and asked him where his swimming partner was.

'It's Miranda, sir,' he said. 'But she's still getting ready.'

Suddenly there was a bloodcurdling cry from the other side of the pool and Miranda burst out of the girls' changing-rooms. She ran along the side of the pool and, when she had reached the deep end, dive-bombed into the water. The splash that she created soaked Mrs Clegg and Mr Skellern to the skin, and Miranda giggled as she surfaced.

Mrs Clegg walked to the edge of the pool and called after Miranda. She was seething with rage and Miranda instantly regretted what she had done. Miranda was ordered out of the water and told to sit by the side of the pool in disgrace. Even Mr Skellern looked disapprovingly at her.

She watched miserably as the younger kids played in the water. At the shallow end the lifeguard was teaching some of the infants how to swim, while at the deep end Arjun and his mates were playing with a large, brightly-coloured ball. She glared at Mrs Clegg, who was helping Liam put on his arm bands at the far end of the pool. It seemed like everyone had forgotten about her. Typical! And all because she'd just wanted a little bit of fun!

Suddenly she heard a shriek from the deep end. Arjun had thrown the ball out of the pool and Mr Skellern had run after it for him. The young student had slipped on the side of the pool and crashed into the water. Arjun started giggling in the water, but Miranda knew something that none of the others did.

'He can't swim!' she cried, and leapt out of her seat.

Already Mr Skellern was struggling in the water and was sinking to the bottom of the pool.

Miranda raced along the poolside and dived into the water. Alerted by the noise, the lifeguard at the shallow end threw himself into the water and started swimming towards Mr Skellern and Miranda with strong, sure strokes.

Miranda reached the panicking Mr Skellern first and started to drag him to the surface. She wrapped her arm around him, trying to keep his mouth above water. But Mr Skellern was too heavy and Miranda felt them both sinking beneath the surface again.

The lifeguard finally reached them and, with Miranda's help, managed to pull Mr Skellern to the side of the pool. Mrs Clegg leant over and helped to drag the student out of the water.

'Are you all right?' she asked.

Mr Skellern nodded, and coughed and spluttered, trying to get his breath back.

'You're lucky Miranda was watching,' the older teacher said.

Mr Skellern turned to Miranda, who was just climbing out of the water after him. He grinned at her. 'Thanks, Miranda,' he panted.

'That's OK,' she said, as if she saved people from

drowning every single day of her life. She looked at Mrs Clegg. 'Can I get back in now?'

Mrs Clegg sighed. After her dive-bombing trick Miranda should have been banned from the water for the rest of the afternoon. But she could hardly refuse her now, especially as she'd just saved a teacher's life.

Mrs Clegg smiled and nodded. Miranda whooped triumphantly and dive-bombed into the water once again.

Chapter Sixteen

'Come on, you lazy lot!' cried Fred Langley above the howl of the wind. 'We've only just started!'

Everyone groaned and looked at the warden. They were all exhausted, even Mrs Sherry and Mr Bamber. It was half-past ten in the morning and they had been walking on the fell for almost an hour. But from the way their legs ached, they might as well have climbed Mount Everest. Mr Langley and Laurie, however, seemed about as tired as if they'd just made a quick trip to the corner shop and back. It must be something to do with all this country air, thought Lee as he helped Roberta up the hill: it made grown-ups quite mad.

'All right, get into your groups now,' Mr Langley ordered. 'It's up to you to tell us which way we go now!'

Barton Wood split into two groups. One was led by Mrs Sherry, the other by Mr Bamber.

Mrs Sherry and her team tried hard to remember all the map-reading tips which Mr Langley had given them yesterday, before the pillow-fight, the appearance of the 'ghost' and getting to sleep at half-past three in the morning.

Most of them could make neither head nor tail of the map, and it was practically impossible for Mr Bamber, who had been hitchhiking his way to Boddington Hall when Mr Langley had given his little talk.

'Don't we go down there?' asked Lyn, and pointed to a spot on the map.

'Don't be daft!' Paul said. 'It would take us two weeks to get there!'

'Besides, we've just come *up* there!' someone else pointed out.

Len Bamber looked all around him, trying to make some connection between the rocks, the hills, the squiggly lines and patches of green and brown on the map. Ten pairs of anxious eyes looked up at him, waiting for the grown-up's words of wisdom.

In fact, Mr Bamber didn't have the slightest clue which way they should go now. From a distance Mr Langley watched him with a mixture of disappointment and amusement. These townsfolk were all the same, he realized. Take them more than fifty metres outside the city limits and they'd have a hard job even to find their nose in front of their face!

Mr Bamber continued to look for a clue as to which direction to go in next. He was just about to admit defeat, when he spotted a bright yellow arrow painted on one of the rocks which lined the path. He looked around quickly, making sure that none of the others from Barton Wood had noticed it. Then he pretended to consult his map again.

'I think we go . . . this way!' he said with certainty.

He started to march off in the direction the arrow indicated and his team followed him, well impressed by his map-reading skills.

Behind him, Mr Langley and Laurie chuckled. They'd both seen Mr Bamber spot the arrows which had been painted at strategic points to help people like him who were hopeless at map-reading. But they weren't going to let on.

After all, Len Bamber was a school governor, and he needed the respect of the children. It wouldn't do for them to know that he'd been holding his map upside down for the last half-hour!

It was noon when they stopped. They could tell it was noon, Fred Langley told them, because the sun was directly overhead in the sky. Mr Bamber knew it was noon because his tummy was rumbling.

They halted for lunch on a tiny hill which had a magnificent view of the surrounding countryside. As the children and Laurie helped to hand out the packed lunches, Mrs Sherry and Mr Langley did a quick head-count.

'We're two missing,' she told Mr Bamber.

'I'll find them,' he said. 'We don't want them getting lost!'

Mrs Sherry laughed as Mr Bamber walked back, retracing their path. She only hoped that there were enough yellow arrows to guide him. Otherwise they'd be missing one school governor too, by the end of the day!

It didn't take Mr Bamber too long to find the two missing children. In a small clearing a little way off, Roberta and Lee were standing by a large tree. With the penknife that he'd been given for his birthday last year Lee was carving his and Roberta's initials into the bark of the tree. Mr Bamber coughed discreetly and the pair of them jumped.

Roberta giggled, but Lee's face was red with embarrassment at having been discovered indulging in such serious sloppiness. Mr Bamber grinned – it reminded him of when he was a boy. That seemed over a thousand years ago now.

'We're all waiting for you, you know,' he said softly.

Lee gulped. 'You're not going to tell anyone, are you?' he asked nervously. If Nicky or Kenny found out how much he fancied Roberta, then they wouldn't stop pulling his leg about it for the rest of their stay at Boddington Hall.

'My lips are sealed,' Mr Bamber promised. 'Now let's get back quickly, before they notice you're gone!'

'Are you all right, Kenny?' Mr Bamber asked as he came and sat down next to him. All during lunch on the hillside Kenny had been sitting a little way off from the others. He looked sad and incredibly fed up.

Kenny grunted, but didn't give an answer.

'Mrs Sherry's had a word with Mr Langley about what happened,' he said. 'I'm sure he wouldn't have said anything if he'd known . . .'

'Don't care if he did,' Kenny said sulkily, although it was clear to Mr Bamber that he did, in fact, care quite a lot.

'You got your spending money, Kenny?' Mr Bamber asked.

Puzzled, Kenny took three one-pound coins out of his pocket. 'I'm going to buy some prezzies,' he said. 'Get my dad and grandad one of them Boddington Hall pens and a tea-towel for me nan.'

Len Bamber took the coins from Kenny's out-stretched hand. 'How much spending money you got now, Kenny?' he asked.

Kenny frowned. 'None – you've got it,' he replied.

Mr Bamber smiled. 'That's the trouble with money,' he said. 'You spend it, you give it away and it's gone.'

Kenny shrugged. What sort of daft game was Bamber playing at now? he wondered.

'Now love's different, Kenny,' he said. 'Sometimes you can give it away and still have loads of it left . . . It don't run out, you know . . .'

Mr Bamber fished around in the top pocket of his cagoule and took out his wallet. He opened it and showed Kenny the small black-and-white photograph inside.

'That's my first wife,' he said. 'She got ill and died just when I had so many plans for us, Kenny; all the places we would have gone to . . . Then I got really lonely. It was years before I met and married Carole – Mrs Bamber now. And I love her, Kenny. But on days like this, with the hills and the trees and you kids, I still think of my first wife and how she would have enjoyed it all. And I still love her, just like I always did.'

Kenny looked strangely at Mr Bamber. It felt weird having a grown-up tell him so much about how he felt. The Councillor got to his feet.

'Love doesn't run out, Kenny,' he said meaningfully, and tossed Kenny his money back. 'Don't worry about love – I bet your dad's got more than enough to go around.'

That night everyone slept like logs. Even Councillor Bamber fell asleep as soon as his head hit his pillow, although that might have had a little to do with the wine he drank with his dinner.

When the children woke up the following morning

they surprised themselves by all wishing that they didn't have to go home. Even though they were all knackered they had to admit that they'd had some great fun. Some of them even asked Mrs Sherry when they could come again.

Even Mr Langley hadn't turned out to be such a bad old codger, once he'd got them off the hill and made sure that they weren't going to put themselves into any danger.

In a funny way he was a bit like Mrs Clegg back at Barton Wood. He might be all frosty and serious most of the time, but deep down they realized that he had a heart of gold. It just went to prove that you could never judge anyone only by appearance. Not that any of them would ever say that to his face, of course.

When they all lined up to say goodbye to Mr Langley and Laurie, they found that they were all wishing they could stay another day. But it was Friday morning now, and the coach was already waiting to take them all back to Barton Wood.

'Bye, kids,' said Laurie as she and Mr Langley helped them on to the coach with their luggage. 'I hope you all had a good time!'

Roberta smiled. She was holding a small teddy bear which Lee had bought for her at Boddington Hall's souvenir shop. 'Oh yes, miss,' she said, 'we had a great time . . .'

Nicky winked at Lee and poked him in the ribs. 'Some of us more than others, eh, Lee?' he said.

Lee sighed. His and Roberta's big secret was out! How was he ever going to live this one down back at Barton Wood?

*

Two hours later, when the coach reached Barton Wood, a collection of parents had already gathered around the school gates for its arrival. Amongst them were Mr Bayfield and Sheila, who had brought Kenny's dad in her car.

She stood a little way back as Kenny got off the coach and Mr Bayfield ran up to greet him. She knew how awkward Kenny must feel having her around; once he and his dad had said their hellos she'd drive them home and then leave them to have some time on their own.

Mr Bayfield grinned down at Kenny and went round to the side of the coach to collect his luggage.

'I got you some presents from the souvenir shop,' Kenny said, as he started to lug his bag to Sheila's waiting car. He dropped the bag on to the ground and unzipped it.

'Leave it now, son,' Mr Bayfield said. 'That can wait for later.'

Kenny shook his head. This was much too important for later: he had to do it now.

He glanced over at Sheila, waiting for them by the car. She would never replace his mum, he knew that. But then he remembered what Mr Bamber had said . . .

'I got some pens for you and Grandad,' he said, and showed his dad the pens with *Boddington Hall* written down the side of them. He pulled out a tea-towel. 'And this is for Gran.'

He looked over once again at Sheila. She was smiling, but at the same time she looked a little sad. Like she's feeling left out; like she knows that she's not one of the family, Kenny thought.

He reached down into his bag, and pulled out a china mug with a picture of Boddington Hall on the side. He carried it over to his dad's girlfriend.

'And this is for you, Sheila,' he said, slightly embarrassed.

Sheila reached down and took the mug. She held it as though it was one of the crown jewels. She smiled down at Kenny and suddenly discovered that there was a lump in her throat.

'Thank you, Kenny,' she said. Kenny grinned.

Mr Bayfield ruffled his son's hair. 'Fish and chips, Kenny?' he asked, and Kenny nodded his head. 'And what do you fancy, Sheila?'

Sheila continued to look gratefully at Kenny. She knew why Kenny had bought her the mug. It was his way of saying sorry for being so selfish before.

'A cup of tea,' she said. 'I fancy a cup of tea in a Boddington Hall mug!'

Smiling and happy, Kenny, his dad and Sheila climbed into the car.

As they drove away Mrs Sherry was met at the main entrance to the school. Her heart sank: there was a very serious and worried look on the deputy head's face. She sighed: she knew that some trouble would happen the minute she left Barton Wood.

'What's up, Jack?' she asked.

'I think we'd better go inside,' he said ominously, and led the way into the school.

Mrs Sherry wondered what Jack Higgins had to tell her. Whatever it was, she was willing to bet that it wasn't going to be good news.

Chapter Seventeen

'For goodness' sake, Joe! Slow down a bit!' Jackie Kerton scolded her husband. Joe was dressed in his trousers and vest and was trying to eat a slice of toast while putting on his shoes and socks at the same time.

'I'm late!' he spluttered in mid-swallow. 'Is that shirt ready yet?'

Jackie switched off the iron and took his shirt off the ironing-board.

'What did your last slave die of?' she asked sarcastically as she handed him his shirt.

'Not getting my clothes ironed on time,' he said, and struggled into the shirt.

'I'll be glad when you've gone to work,' said Jackie.

Joe had been moody ever since coming home on Friday night. He'd told her that the maintenance engineers had finally arrived at Barton Wood to examine the subsidence on the sports field. And they'd found something more than just holes in the field. A dirty great crack halfway down the wall of the school hall, in fact. That was the bad news that Mr Higgins had given Mrs Sherry when she arrived back from Boddington Hall.

'Well, excuse me,' he said as he tried to digest his last piece of toast. 'Sorry for not being the life and soul, but I might be out of a job come the end of term!'

Jackie laughed, not sure whether her husband was being serious or not. 'Don't be daft!' she said.

'If the school shuts down then I'm on the dole,' he told her, deadly serious. 'Then where would we be?'

'The maintenance engineers have just discovered a crack in one of the walls, that's all,' Jackie said quite calmly. She still couldn't see what all the fuss was about.

'Cracks don't appear for no reason,' Joe said, and grabbed his bag.

'You always blow everything out of all proportion!' Jackie said. 'For goodness' sake, stop worrying!'

Joe opened the door and stormed out of the kitchen. 'We'll both be worrying if the school closes down!' he cried back as he jumped on his bicycle and started to cycle off down the front path.

So worried was he about getting into school on time that he didn't notice Miranda, who had come over from her own house to see why Joe and Jackie were having such an argy-bargy so early in the morning. It wasn't like them at all, she knew, so she reckoned it must be something really important.

She had also wanted to tell Joe that Mrs Sherry was going to present her with an award today for saving Skellern's life in the swimming-pool. But this piece of news was even *more* exciting.

So Barton Wood was going to be closed down! For good, for keeps, for ever and ever! Now there was a really juicy bit of gossip for Miranda to spread around the school for Monday morning! The week was getting off to a great start already!

A sense of gloom hung over the staffroom at Barton

Wood. Mr Skellern, Mrs Clegg and Miss Richards were all clearly very worried; after all, Mrs Sherry had never called a staff meeting before classes began.

Only Olive Swainsgate knew why the meeting had been called, but Mrs Sherry had sworn her to secrecy. She only wished that Mrs Sherry would turn up soon: if she didn't, she was sure she was going to burst out and reveal the secret.

'Do you think that this staff meeting's about the school trip?' Miss Richards asked. 'You don't suppose they lost any of the kids, do you?'

Mrs Clegg chuckled. 'There's one or two I wish they had . . .'

Mrs Swainsgate agreed. 'Nicky Power and Lee Rayner would be top of my list,' she admitted.

'They're all right,' Mr Skellern protested, and then reconsidered. 'Well, they do have their moments . . .'

The door to the staffroom clicked open and Mrs Sherry and Mr Higgins walked in. That was a bad sign in itself, if the bad news had to be told by two of them. They sat down.

'I've called this staff meeting so that Jack can put you all in the picture,' Mrs Sherry said. 'A bit of a problem has come up . . .'

Mr Higgins continued. 'As you know, we had a couple of council bods here last week to look at the holes in the playing field . . .'

'So when are they going to fill them in?' asked Miss Richards.

'I'm afraid it's not as simple as that,' said Mr Higgins, and Miss Richards shook her head wearily. No, she hadn't supposed that it would be: nothing was ever that simple at Barton Wood.

'There have been some new developments,' Mr Higgins revealed. 'A crack has appeared along the wall of the school hall . . .'

Mrs Clegg couldn't see what all the fuss was about. She often had cracks in the wall of her old house; it was nothing a bit of Polyfilla couldn't get rid of.

'Are you saying that these two things are connected?' she asked.

'The council are sending another maintenance engineer around today,' Mr Higgins said. 'Until we receive his report we mustn't start jumping to any conclusions.'

'So what do we tell the children?' asked Mr Skellern.

'Nothing at all!' Mrs Sherry said. 'I don't want any silly rumours being passed around.' She sighed. 'You know what children can be like . . .'

'So that's it,' Miranda told Esi as they arrived for school that morning. 'The school's closing down! It's definite – I heard Joe Kerton say so!'

Esi called Lee, Nicky, Kenny and Lyn over to tell them the good news. They all cheered; as Lee said, it was 'fan-bloomin'-tastic'.

'But why's it closing down?' asked Kenny.

Miranda shrugged. 'How should I know?' she said. Surely it was enough for Kenny that Barton Wood was closing down? Did he really have to know the reason as well?

'I know what's happened,' said Esi. Five puzzled faces looked questioningly at her. 'It's something *dead* mysterious!'

'Like what?' asked Lyn.

'Like the Roman ghost!' Esi replied. 'He's spreading his evil forces all around the school. Maybe he's summoned up a whole legion of other ghostly Romans to run us all out of Barton Wood!'

'Don't talk daft!' Kenny said, but by his side Lyn seemed very worried.

'They're probably all around us now,' Esi continued in her best spooky voice. 'They're just waiting to put their icy fingers around your neck, Lyn!'

Lyn squealed with horror, as she felt two clammy hands slip around her neck. She turned around, convinced that the ghost of Barton Wood had finally caught up with her. Miranda was standing behind her, a mischievous look on her face.

'Gotcha!' she said, and winked.

Darren stared down at his feet, at the waste-paper basket, in fact at anything other than Mrs Sherry's accusing stare and the objects on her desk. He knew when he was well and truly nicked and he didn't like it one little bit.

'Is everything here?' Mrs Sherry asked, and indicated the watch, goggles and Victorian fan which had gone missing, and which she now knew had been stolen by Darren. Darren said yes.

'Why were you taking all these things, Darren?' she asked, and pointed down to his wrist. 'You've already got a watch of your own. Why did you want Mr Skellern's?'

'I just saw it on the sink in the toilets and thought . . . well, it made me feel good to take it . . .' It was a pretty feeble excuse and Darren knew it.

'But why?' Mrs Sherry asked, but Darren couldn't

give an answer. 'It's very wrong to steal and you should know that. You've upset a lot of people.' She sighed and gathered the stolen objects up, putting them in a drawer in her desk for safekeeping. 'This has to stop, Darren. I'm sure your father and mother will be very upset about this.'

At the mention of his mum and dad Darren finally looked up at Mrs Sherry. 'Please don't tell *them*,' he begged her.

Mrs Sherry shook her head. 'I'm sorry,' she said firmly, 'but we must. If you do something really wrong, Darren, then you must face the consequences . . .

Of all the people who had been told that Barton Wood might have to close down, Jackie Kerton was perhaps the least worried. In her marriage she had always been the sensible one; Joe, on the other hand, was like a big kid and always went over the top.

So while Joe was sitting in his cubby-hole of an office worrying about the future and Miranda and Esi were spreading the news all around the school, Jackie did the most sensible thing in the world: she went shopping.

On the Pennington Road she bumped into Mrs Pudsey, Miranda's mother. The two neighbours had never really chatted before, apart from a quick 'hello' when they saw each other in the street. But now that it was common knowledge that Jackie was going to be a mother, Mrs Pudsey felt obliged to ask Jackie how she felt.

'I'll be glad to get rid of this morning sickness,' Jackie laughed. She was surprised when she saw Mrs Pudsey scowl.

'I was sick every blooming day with Miranda,' she growled. 'She made me sick then – and she makes me sick now . . .'

'She's not a bad lass,' Jackie said cheerfully. She thought that Mrs Pudsey was only joking. 'She's always as good as gold when she's round at our place.'

'At least it keeps her out of my hair,' Mrs Pudsey said, although it was clear to Jackie that she had unknowingly hit on a sore point. 'She does nowt but pester me.'

'Maybe Miranda just wants a little bit of attention?' Jackie suggested tactfully. 'You don't seem to spend much time with her yourself . . .'

'It's none of your damned business what I do or don't do!' Mrs Pudsey snapped. 'It's easy for you. You play with her for ten minutes and then you send her packing when you've had enough! You don't have to live with her!'

Jackie was taken aback by Mrs Pudsey's sudden outburst. 'I'm sorry,' she said. 'I had no right to say what I did.'

Mrs Pudsey shrugged, and softened a little bit. 'Well, you might have a point,' she admitted.

Jackie looked up, interested, as Mrs Pudsey continued.

'Things haven't been the same since Stevie, Miranda's little brother, died. He was right sickly from being born and he left us when he was only a few months old . . .'

Jackie remembered that Miranda had called her puppy Stevie: now she knew why.

'Miranda was just coming up to her fifth birthday.

And I was so angry when that child died that I couldn't stand the sight of Miranda,' Mrs Pudsey confessed. 'I knew I was in the wrong, but it's too late now. She's locked me out like she's scared of me.'

'I'm sure she isn't –'

'She is,' Mrs Pudsey insisted. 'And I'm scared of her too. I don't know how to talk to her at all.'

Jackie laid a hand on Mrs Pudsey's shoulder. Suddenly a lot of things had become clear to her. She reminded Mrs Pudsey about the presentation that Mrs Sherry was going to make to Miranda that afternoon.

'Are you going to go?' she asked.

Mrs Pudsey shook her head. 'She wouldn't expect me to . . .' she said.

Jackie smiled. It wasn't a matter of what people expected, she knew. It was a matter of what people *wanted* . . . And what people *needed* . . .

The atmosphere was electric. Mrs Sherry had called the lunchtime break ten minutes earlier than usual and now everyone, including the teachers and Councillor Bamber, who was here on one of his regular visits, had gathered in the hall.

Wild rumours had been flying around the school all morning, started by Miranda and Esi. Several infants had even come into the office to ask Mrs Swainsgate if it really was true that Barton Wood was closing down for good; and, if so, could they please go home right now.

Mrs Sherry realized that she had to introduce some damage limitation before things got completely out of hand. If she didn't stop the rumours right now, then she knew that tomorrow morning it would be the parents who would be knocking on her office door to ask when the school was closing down.

'Before we start lunch I think that we'd all better get something in perspective,' she began, and looked pointedly at Mr Bamber. Kenny Bayfield had told him only half an hour ago that the entire school was falling down, and since then he'd been running around the place like a headless chicken.

'Let me tell you definitely that Barton Wood is not closing down.'

There were a few boos from the back of the hall, which she chose to ignore.

'There is, however, a problem with the wall,' she said, and looked behind her. The crack which the maintenance engineer had spotted last week seemed to have grown. Now it stretched from the ceiling to almost halfway down the wall.

'At this stage no one knows what's causing it, but some gentlemen from the council are making a thorough investigation of the building. If Barton Wood was unsafe then I would have personally closed the school down. So until we hear any more news, could we please call a halt to these silly rumours!'

'I know what we can do,' Paul said after lunch, 'we can get Miranda to fix the school!'

Miranda, who was dreaming about the presentation ceremony which was due to happen in half an hour's time, asked him what rubbish he was talking now.

'Who need the Super Mario Brothers when we've got Super Miranda to help us?' Paul said to the rest of the class. 'She rescues drowning teachers from swimming-pools – she saves schools from falling down!'

Miranda punched him on the arm, but secretly she was rather pleased with all the attention. She loved being taken notice of.

'I wish I'd saved Mr Skellern,' Lyn said, and hugged herself. She'd fancied him since the very first day he had walked into Cleggie's class.

'Hang on,' said Nicky. 'We don't want to save the school from falling down, do we?'

As usual, Lee agreed with him. 'If it shuts we don't have to go to school any more!'

Roberta shook her head. Boys could be really soft at times, she thought. 'If they shut Barton Wood we'd be sent to other schools.'

Nicky hadn't thought of that. He shut up and started to think about what would happen to him if Barton Wood was closed down. Funnily enough, he found he didn't like the idea at all.

'I don't want to go anywhere else,' Lyn said. For a start, if she was moved to another school there'd be no Mr Skellern to drool over. She wouldn't have minded escaping from the ghost of Barton Wood though.

'My mum and dad reckon this is a good school,' Paul said. 'What if we get sent to a rough one?'

'The teachers are really good here,' Roberta agreed.

'Swot!' Nicky said. He couldn't believe what he was hearing. All his mates were suddenly standing up for the teachers!

'It would be like starting school all over again,'

154

said Esi. 'No friends ... feeling dead lonely ... strange teachers ...'

Lee got the point and glanced over at Mrs Clegg and Mr Skellern, who were chatting by the teacher's table. 'Yeah, even stranger than this lot ...'

Miranda stared down at all the people in the school hall. All her mates were there and all the teachers too. There was even a photographer from the *Irwell Valley Recorder*.

And they had all come just to see her! To see her, Miranda Pudsey, up here on the stage! She felt very proud and, even better, very important.

'Miranda showed great quickness of thought during a potentially dangerous situation at the swimming-pool last week,' Mrs Sherry announced to everyone, even though they all knew the story by now. Miranda had wasted no time in telling everyone how she had heroically saved Mr Skellern from drowning.

As Mrs Sherry continued with her speech the door at the back of the hall opened. Miranda couldn't believe her eyes when she saw Jackie Kerton walk in, followed by her mother! Mrs Pudsey was the very last person Miranda would have expected to come to see her get her award.

Mrs Sherry finished her speech and presented Miranda with a merit medal which she pinned carefully on to her jumper. The whole hall burst into applause and cheers. But Miranda couldn't take her eyes off her mum at the back of the hall.

Mr Skellern came up to her and gave her his own special present – an expensive-looking painting set.

Miranda nodded her thanks and the hall burst into applause again, this time led by Mr Skellern himself.

Miranda's heart swelled with pride and joy. But it was not the applause or the cheering that was now making her happier than she'd been in a long, long time.

It was her mum at the back of the hall. She was clapping and cheering louder than anyone else there.

Her mum had actually come to school to watch her get her medal! Miranda was gobsmacked. Her mum had come to share in her happiness. Her mum had come to show her support.

And that was the best prize Miranda Pudsey had ever had in her whole life.

Mrs James nervously handed Mr Higgins a cup of tea. She was very worried. The deputy head had arrived at the hairdressing salon, which she owned with her husband, about half an hour ago.

He'd mentioned on the telephone that he needed to talk to her about Darren, and she had thought that perhaps he'd been misbehaving in class. Nothing could have prepared her for the fact that Darren was a thief.

'Will you be calling the police in?' she asked.

Mr Higgins smiled and reassured her that he wanted to keep this a private matter between themselves. Both Mrs and Mr James sighed with relief.

'His classmates don't know it was Darren,' Mr Higgins said, 'and I'd like to keep it that way . . .'

They were sitting in the back room of the hairdressing salon, which was piled high to the ceiling with supplies of hairdressing products. It was obvious that the Jameses put a lot of time and effort into their business. The notice on the front door of the salon showed that on some days it was open until eight o'clock at night.

'Do Darren and Roberta sit in here every night while you're out in the salon working?' Mr Higgins asked.

'We try to make fewer bookings in the evenings,' Mrs James said, 'so that one of us can take them home. But sometimes if we're really busy they might have to hang on for a bit.'

'We've had to work hard in building this business up,' Mr James said, a little defensively. 'But we've not neglected our children.'

'I wasn't suggesting you had,' said Mr Higgins. 'But we all want to find out why Darren seems to be seeking attention . . . Roberta's an outgoing child, but perhaps Darren needs a bit more time to get used to you both being so busy. Maybe he needs a little extra attention – to ensure that work *doesn't* come first for you both . . .'

'Now, look, our kids get all the attention they need,' Mr James retorted angrily. But deep inside he knew that Mr Higgins was right.

'I'll give him a little extra attention at school,' Mr Higgins said, and suggested that the Jameses did the same thing for him at home. 'And let's hope that that will work.'

After all, he told them as he left, there was no doubt that Mr and Mrs James loved Darren. But like all young children, he needed to be shown that they did. Darren wasn't a born thief: all he really wanted was to be noticed.

Mrs Sherry looked up anxiously as the man from the

council walked into her office. He'd been inspecting the school premises all afternoon.

'So what's the verdict?' she asked. She hoped she sounded confident. Inside she was scared of what he might have discovered.

The man consulted the clipboard he was carrying – all casual-like, Mrs Sherry noticed, as if he couldn't care less whether Barton Wood was going to remain standing or fall down tomorrow.

He wasn't being unkind or unthinking, she knew; it was just that he hadn't spent the last year of his life trying to make the school into one the teachers, pupils and parents could all feel proud of.

'There's obviously a problem with the land the school's built on,' he began. 'It might be old mine-workings. But to be certain we're going to have to do some tests.'

That sounded ominous. 'What sort of tests?' Mrs Sherry asked.

'We'll have to drill holes through the foundations of the school.'

That seemed simple enough, Mrs Sherry thought.

'Well, half-term's only a week away, so presumably you can wait till after the fête,' she said. 'We have quite a few children with asthma here – the drilling will throw up a lot of dust . . .'

'I don't think you understand,' said the council man. 'If I were you I wouldn't worry about any short-term disruption.'

'You wouldn't?' Mrs Sherry could feel some very bad news coming.

'If there is a mineshaft under here,' he said, 'then the school will have to close down for good!'

Chapter Eighteen

The day of the Barton Wood school fête dawned bright and clear. Even the weather, for once, seemed to be on the school's side and the sun shone through the windows out of a nearly cloudless sky, making the multicoloured streams of bunting and the extravagantly decorated stalls seem even more bright and inviting.

In the hall there were stalls of every size and description. There was a hoop-la stall, where if you were lucky you could win yourself one of the goldfish which the local pet shop had donated. There was even a stall where, if you managed to pin the tail on a cardboard donkey while blindfolded, you could win one of several cuddly toys, which had been given to Barton Wood by the manager of the local toyshop.

Mr Vasisht had also given items from his shop to be sold. And Kim's mum and dad, determined not to be outdone, had donated vouchers for free takeaways from their restaurant, which were to go into the raffle to be held later that afternoon.

Outside, the playground, the teachers' car-park and the sports field were almost completely covered with even more stalls. There were cake stalls and lucky dips; stalls selling plants and second-hand books, records and CDs; there was a toy stall, and a white elephant stall, where people tried to sell things which they no longer needed.

The dinner ladies had been persuaded to come in

on a Saturday and set up a hot-dog stand, and some parents were helping them fry the onions and sausages on large, sizzling platters.

A large platform had also been erected in the playground. It had been decked out in streamers, ribbons and coloured balloons, and an enormous poster told everyone that the highlight of the day – the fancy-dress competition – was going to be held at three o'clock sharp.

It was still only twelve noon. Most of the parents and children wouldn't be arriving until two o'clock, when Councillor Bamber would officially declare the fête open, yet the school was already packed with children and their parents, eager to grab some bargains or try their luck at the hoop-la stall before the crowds arrived.

As she watched everyone arrive, from her office windows, Mrs Sherry knew that this should be one of the happiest moments of her time at Barton Wood. The fête was going to be a great success, and all the money raised today would go into the school fund to buy more books and stationery, and maybe improve the facilities at the school.

So why was she feeling so miserable?

She turned to Mrs Clegg. 'I don't think I've ever felt so professionally depressed in my life,' she told her.

Mrs Clegg smiled sympathetically, and also looked out through the window at the goings-on outside. 'All the fun of the fair – when we're going to be closed down . . .'

'We *might* be closed down!' Mrs Sherry reminded her. The men from the council weren't due for another few hours yet – and no one knew what they would find until they started their investigation into the school grounds.

Mrs Sherry smiled: Esi would have probably told her that they'd find the body of the Roman 'ghost'. Mrs Sherry almost hoped that that was all they would find.

'We're *likely* to be closed,' Mrs Clegg corrected her gently as the door to the office opened and Jack Higgins came in.

He saw the miserable faces of his two fellow teachers and pulled an equally miserable face himself. 'What's this?' he joked. 'The Long Face Competition?'

'No, the Forced Smile Competition,' said Mrs Clegg, who was just as worried as Mrs Sherry. If Barton Wood closed it might not be that easy for her to find another job at a school she liked as much. She was over fifty, after all.

Mr Higgins sat on Mrs Sherry's desk. 'Are you going to make an announcement?' he asked. 'I mean, all the money we make today is going to go into the school fund. We might not have a school to spend it on!'

'I've decided to say something at the opening,' she told him. 'I hope it won't spoil everybody's fun . . .'

Mr Higgins was in charge of the PA system on the outdoor platform, and he asked Mrs Sherry if she could come and check if the sound level was OK for her speech. She was about to follow him out to the platform, when they heard a very familiar voice boom out from the loudspeakers.

'There was a little monkey,
Got hold of a bottle of rum,
He tried to swing from tree to tree,
But he landed on his –'

'Lee Rayner!' cried Mr Higgins, and then fell about laughing. 'The little beggar's got hold of my PA equipment!'

Len Bamber looked around the stalls and games of the Barton Wood fête. He could hardly move because of children and their parents. There was no doubt about it – Chris Sherry had done them all proud. This had to be the most successful fête he had ever seen, and it was a real crying shame that it was probably going to be the last one too.

Len Bamber knew what they all said about him behind his back, but he didn't really mind. He'd started out as a young man playing for Preston North End, way back in those glory days when they'd been a really great team. He'd even made it to the England squad.

When he'd got too old to play football any more he'd hung up his boots and become a local councillor. But all his council work, and even his days with PNE, meant nothing compared to being Chair of Governors of Barton Wood school. He loved this school, loved these kids, and now it seemed as if he was going to lose them all.

'It's a bad lookout, isn't it?' he said to Mrs Sherry in the school playground. She was standing by the side of the stage, looking over the notes she had made for her opening speech. 'I can tell you it's knocked me into touch . . .'

'That's not like you, Len,' she said.

'This school has been my baby,' he said. 'I've held it by the hand every step of the way . . . and I can't imagine losing it . . .'

Mrs Sherry tried to be cheerful. 'C'mon, Len,' she said. 'It's not all over until the final whistle!'

'Whatever is going to happen we'll have to tell the children and their parents something.'

'I've come to the same conclusion myself,' Mrs Sherry said, and showed him the piece of paper on which she'd been jotting down some notes.

'*I'll* do it at the opening,' Len Bamber said, and looked at his watch.

There was only about fifteen minutes left before the fête was to be declared officially open. He took a pen and a notebook out of his inside blazer pocket and started to make his own notes.

Mrs Sherry smiled. 'You're very good, Len,' she said, 'and a head couldn't ask for a more supportive Chair of Governors.' She took the pen and notebook from him. 'But *I'll* do it – *I'll* tell them!'

Len Bamber might have his heart in the right place, she thought. But knowing him he'd probably mess it all up and convince the parents that there was a major earthquake due in Barton Wood and not just a little subsidence!

Mrs Sherry took a deep breath and climbed on to the stage. Everyone was looking at her: schoolchildren, their mums and dads, stepmums and stepdads, their grandparents, their mates. Several of the children were wearing fancy dress. Kenny and Paul had both come dressed as Julius Caesar. In keeping with the

Roman theme Mandy had come as the great warrior queen Boadicea, and had attached cardboard 'blades' to the spokes of her wheelchair.

It was now two o'clock, the official opening time of Barton Wood fête, and this was going to be the hardest speech Mrs Sherry had ever made in her entire life.

'Thank you for coming,' she began, 'and thank you to Councillor Bamber, who will officially open the fête.'

A cheer went up from the audience. It was so loud that it drowned out the noise of the van which had just driven through the school gates. Mrs Sherry saw it, however, and read the sign on its side: *P. J. Kingsland – Structural Repairs*. Her heart sank.

'I think I had better explain what's going on,' she said, and a few of the parents nodded their heads in agreement. They all knew about the rumours of course, and Mrs Sherry had even gone to the trouble of making sure that they had all received duplicated letters about the matter.

'When I sent you those letters,' she continued, 'we knew that Barton Wood had some structural problems. But we didn't think that they were serious. We've since been told that test holes need to be drilled through the school's foundations to find out what's going on underneath. And it appears that this won't be completed by the end of next week's half-term holiday!'

In the crowd Lee let out a mighty cheer. That meant that they'd all have an extra-long holiday!

Mrs Sherry smiled at Lee. 'Now, that might sound good news to some of you, but it could go on much,

much longer. So for the sake of health and safety I'm going to have to make arrangements for your children to go to other schools in the area.'

Lee looked at Nicky, Miranda, Paul, Esi, Kenny and all the others. Their faces were all white with worry. Leave Barton Wood? Go to another school? Leave all their friends behind? Suddenly no one felt like cheering any more.

'What do you think the problem is?' asked Paul's dad from the crowd.

'Yeah, Barton Wood's not been open a year yet,' said Gran Bayfield.

Councillor Bamber came forward and took the microphone from Mrs Sherry. 'There's some movement in the ground under the school,' he said, 'and they reckon that there must be an old mineshaft down there.'

The parents began to mutter amongst themselves. This sounded serious.

'There's no need to worry, though,' Len Bamber reassured them. 'It's just an old mineshaft. Half of Britain is built over old mine tunnels.'

'Stuff and nonsense!' came a voice from the crowd.

Mr Bamber peered into the assembly. It was old Albert Dawson, the man who had come to give Mr Higgins's class a talk on the old Victorian mine.

'You're talking baloney!' he cried. 'You're talking a heap of old nutty slack!'

Mr Bamber laughed at Albert. Since his speech Albert had started work as the lollipop man who helped the kids from Barton Wood cross the road on their way to school. Mr Bamber also recalled Mrs Sherry telling him that Albert had taken care of Scratch, the puppy that was once Nicky's.

'Do you mind?' Mr Bamber said snottily. 'I'm saying what I've been told by experts!'

'All I'm trying to say is –' Albert began, but he was silenced by some of the parents. They wanted to hear what the School Governor had to say. They didn't have the time to listen to the ramblings of an old lollipop man.

Albert stomped away, a dark frown on his brow. Let Len Bamber say what he liked up there on the stage, he thought.

Whatever was under the ground, beneath Barton Wood school, Albert Dawson knew for sure that it wasn't a mineshaft!

Chapter Nineteen

Nicky ran through the allotments, not caring how many carefully-tended vegetable plots he trampled underfoot. He crushed Grandad Bayfield's leeks and carrots as he raced towards the old shack. It was the shack where he had first hidden Scratch, earlier in the term when he'd had that daft idea of rescuing his dad from the nick. As he approached the old hut he heard Scratch bark a welcome. Old Albert, who was sitting on an upturned bucket, looking dejected, glanced up as Nicky ran over to him.

'I knew you'd be here, Albert!' Nicky panted. He was out of breath after having run all the way from school. 'Them men from the council! They've gone and got the ropes up! They've got the signs out saying "Unsafe building. Keep out"!'

Albert sneered. The council men had wasted no time then. But what did *they* know? They were probably only playing safe: he bet they didn't have any idea what was really going on underground at Barton Wood. Not like him, anyway.

'That's a load of old baloney!' he said.

'Have you got proof?' Nicky asked urgently. Albert nodded.

'Well, if you know something, then you've got to make them listen!' Nicky said.

'They've had their chance,' said Albert sulkily. All of a sudden he reminded Nicky of Miranda. She sulked like that when she wasn't getting her own way and when no one was paying her any attention.

'If you've really got proof and you're not just soundin' off, you've got to tell them, Albert!' Nicky insisted.

'Leave it!' Albert said. 'They had their chance to listen to me. Now it's their funeral.'

Nicky knelt down on the ground and looked up at Albert's old and lined face. 'No, Albert,' he said seriously. 'It's *my* funeral . . . I never reckoned I'd go so much on any school . . .'

Albert grunted, but continued to listen to Nicky.

'If Barton Wood closes and I have to go to Pennington, then I'll lose everything,' Nicky said.

'Like what?' Albert asked.

'Like my mates,' Nicky said. 'Like Scratch here, or like Old Mother Sherry . . .'

He paused for a second, thinking of the times Mrs Sherry had looked out for him, even when he'd been caught nicking stuff from Mr Vasisht's store. 'I'll miss feeling like someone gives a ha'penny about me . . . I'll miss you, you silly old beggar . . .'

Albert laughed awkwardly. It was obvious that Nicky's words had touched him. It had only been since he'd given that talk on the Barton Wood coalmine that he'd been working as a lollipop man, but in no time at all he'd got on really well with all the kids at Barton Wood. He'd even taught them all how to play dibsies! They'd made him feel young again. And when you were pushing seventy, then that was something to feel grateful for!

'How do you think all the kids are going to feel if the school's pulled down?' Nicky asked him.

'Over the moon . . .'

'Then that shows how much you know!' said Nicky. He was getting angry now. 'We all go on about how much we hate the school – me, Lee, Kenny, Miranda – but Barton Wood was built for us. We were the *first* kids through that door . . . I fit in there, don't you see?'

He stood up and tugged at the sleeve of Albert's jacket. 'So come on, Albert. Tell us! Tell us and save the school!'

Mrs Sherry looked on sadly as the stallholders started to pack up their stalls. Everything had been sold, all the goldfish and cuddly toys had been won or given away, and the fancy-dress competition had been won by two of the infants.

It was the end of the school fête and the beginning of the half-term holiday. And what was more, it looked like the end of Barton Wood School for good. In the distance she could hear the council workers as they began to drill holes in the school's foundations. She'd had a private word with one of them. He hadn't held out much hope: if she wanted his opinion, then it looked as if the school would have to be pulled down.

Some of the infants were crying; even the normally bright and cheerful Richard Skellern looked miserable.

Mrs Sherry looked sadly over at the school building. She'd spent almost a year trying to make Barton Wood work, and now here she was, defeated at last by a damned hole in the ground! It just wasn't fair. But then who said that life was ever supposed to be fair?

Sighing, she climbed up on to the platform for one last time. She owed it to the parents, the children and the teachers who had had so much faith in her, to say goodbye.

She gazed out at the crowd of faces who had stopped what they were doing to listen to her. Mr Bamber joined her on stage, followed by the rest of the teachers. He called everyone to silence.

Mrs Sherry took a deep breath. She began what was probably the most difficult speech of her whole career.

'Friends of the school, I'd like to thank you all for your help at the fête,' she said. It was hard to keep her voice steady. 'I don't know yet what we've raised for the school fund, but whatever it is it'll be put into a trust for . . . for whenever . . . for whatever happens. I'll be writing to you all with the details of your new schools as soon as I can. Meanwhile have a restful half-term . . .'

Suddenly there was a commotion at the back of the crowd and Nicky pushed his way through, pulling Albert behind him. On the stage Len Bamber groaned: he thought he'd seen the last of that blessed lollipop man!

'Miss, Albert's got something important to tell you!' Nicky shouted.

Mr Bamber groaned again and looked at his watch.

Mrs Sherry looked curiously at Albert. So did all the other teachers. She leant down and helped the old man up on to the platform.

Albert was suddenly aware that everyone was looking at him – parents, kids, teachers; they were eagerly waiting for him to speak. He cleared his throat and addressed the crowd.

'That crack is never from the mining,' he said. 'Neither are those holes.' He pointed over to where the workmen had roped off the school building. 'They can dig till Domesday, but they won't find any mineshaft under this school!'

A flicker of hope appeared in Mrs Sherry's eyes. She told Albert to continue.

'I worked on maintenance at the colliery till it closed and I know those workings like the back of my hand,' he told them. 'They talked about digging under here, but they never got round to it . . .'

'What is it then?' demanded Len Bamber. '*Something's* made those holes, hasn't it?'

'It's that ghost, that Roman ghost!' Esi cried out from the crowd.

Some of the grown-ups in the crowd tried to shush Esi, but Albert laughed.

'The lass is right in a way,' he said. In the crowd Esi stuck her tongue out at those who'd told her to shut up.

'It's the Roman villa,' Albert revealed. 'My father told me about it. They dug round here a hundred years back trying to find where it was. They thought there'd be some treasure, but they didn't find a brass farthing . . .'

Esi's face fell. 'So there never was a ghost,' she said.

Even Lyn, who had lived in terror of the ghost since he had first been mentioned, looked disappointed.

'My guess is that the old Victorians never filled it in properly,' Albert said. 'I reckon that they can sort all this out with no danger. And Barton Wood will be standing in a hundred years' time!'

A massive cheer went up from the crowd. Miranda, Esi, Lyn, Kenny, Paul and Lee all joined in. On the stage Mr Bamber and the teachers applauded Mrs Sherry as she walked up to Albert and gave him a grateful peck on the cheek. Then she turned to address her audience.

She looked at all the happy faces before her. This was what being at a school was all about, she thought. When the going got tough they all pulled together, and they all looked out for each other. Sure enough, at times they might not even be able to stand the sight of one another. But Barton Wood was about sharing – about sharing the good times as well as the bad.

Yes, she realized, they all had their differences. But they also all had one thing in common. She looked back at the school building. She was going to have the time of her life telling those workmen to get their drills out of her school.

No, not *her* school. *Our* school.

She turned to face her audience again.

'Well,' she said, struggling to make herself heard above the cheering, 'it looks like Barton Wood is back in business!'

three seven eleven
Chris and Bernard Ashley

For Kenny, Jordan, Miranda, Kompel and the other pupils of the new school, the best days of their lives are about to come – or are they?

For who has broken into the nursery and what has happened to Esi's treasured photo album? Will the time capsule stay buried and who will win the big match?